HEAD

ABOVE

WATER

HEAD ABOVE WATER

s . l . r o t t m a n

PEACHTREE
ATLANTA

Also by S. L. Rottman
Hero
Rough Waters

ȣ

A Freestone Publication

Published by
PEACHTREE PUBLISHERS, LTD.
494 Armour Circle NE
Atlanta, Georgia 30324

www.peachtree-online.com

Text © 1999 by S. L. Rottman
Jacket illustration © 1999 by Suzy Schultz

Jacket and book design by Loraine M. Balcsik
Composition by Melanie M. McMahon

Manufactured in the United States of America

10 9 8 7 6 5 4 3 2

Library of Congress Cataloging-in-Publication Data
Rottman, S.L.
   Head above water / S.L. Rottman. -- 1st ed.
      p.   cm.
   Summary: Skye, a high school junior, tries to find the time for both family obligations and personal interests, which include caring for her brother who has Down syndrome, dating her first boyfriend, and swimming competitively.
   ISBN 1-56145-185-1
   [1. High schools Fiction.   2. Schools Fiction.   3. Down syndrome Fiction.   4. Mentally handicapped Fiction.   5. Swimming Fiction.]
   I. Title.
   PZ7.R7534Hd   1999
   [Fic]--dc21   99-26030
                                                                        CIP

Thanks again to my family,
for their continuing love and support.

To Christie and Gail,
who offered wisdom, insight, criticism,
and years of friendship.

To the Deer Creek Class of 2002,
a gifted bunch of 7th graders.
May your individual talents take you far.

Chapter One

W hen I got to the locker room, everyone else was already on
deck. I made record time changing, but by the time I got out
there, the rest of the team was in the water. I tossed my bag
on a bench and went directly to Coach Sullivan.

"Sorry I'm late, Coach," I said, my heart pounding. This was the first
time I had ever been late to practice.

"Excused?" he asked without looking up from his clipboard.

"No."

"Stretch out and get in. Stay late tonight."

I nodded and went through the stretches as quickly as I could without
leaving out any of the essential ones. Coach would know if I skipped too
many of them. And, I knew the importance of stretching before getting in
the water. The last thing I wanted to do was hurt myself by doing something stupid.

Hannah and I shared the distance lane with Deb and Christie. They
were already halfway through warm-up, so I waited for an opening to get
in and swim with them.

I took a breath and did a lazy dive into the water. It felt jarringly cool,
as it always did. I knew the goose bumps would be gone before I had
completed my first lap. I held a tight streamline, kicked short and strong,
and got nearly fifteen yards out from the wall before I came up for a
breath. Settling into my rhythm only took three or four strokes.

I had been swimming for so long, I could almost detach my mind
from my body. Breathe, duck, turn, push, kick, pull, breathe, pull, pull,

breathe, pull, pull, breathe, pull, pull. It had an almost hypnotic effect. I lived to swim. To feel the water slide down from my head to my toes. To watch the bottom of the pool slide by effortlessly. To listen to my breathing and the water splashing and to feel my hand slice through the still water in front of me, parting it and using it to my advantage. For me there was no other sport in the world.

When I was halfway down the pool and turned my head to breathe, I knew I'd see Sunny sitting in his spot on the bleachers. I always knew where to look for him, always knew he'd be there. I tried to picture what he had been wearing this morning when we left for school. It was a game I played, testing my memory, to see if I could remember. Today I couldn't. I had too many other things on my mind.

I turned my head, and there he was, shaggy blond head bent over his books, struggling with his homework. He was wearing his favorite Westwood High sweatshirt, which was a blue that brought out the color of his eyes.

I felt terrible about being late for practice. My best friend, Jenny, had insisted on talking to me after school about something really important. I had to admit she had some exciting news. She wanted to tell me that Mike Banner had been asking her boyfriend about me. I had heard that Mike and DeAnna Garcia, a senior and a varsity cheerleader, had broken up at the end of the summer, right before school started, but I had never dreamed he would be interested in me. Jenny was sure he was going to ask me out.

Forget it, I told myself. *You've got too many other things to focus on.*

I turned my head back down, and I groaned out loud in the water when I released my breath. Sometimes I scream, if it's been a really bad day. The great thing about screaming underwater is that no one else can hear. And when I'm really angry or frustrated, I can tear through the water, beating it up, and by the time I finish a workout, I'm too tired to be angry anymore.

Pull, breathe, pull, pull, breathe, pull, pull, breathe, pull, pull, breathe, duck, turn, push, kick, pull. I put myself on autopilot and followed Christie's feet in front of me, staying just a few feet behind her toes, knowing it was Christie from the way her feet crossed over every third kick.

I have a fair amount of homework tonight, so I'll give myself an hour and a half. And Sunny will need help. He has a test coming up in Western Civ, so I'll have to help him study. Another hour for quizzing him. Maybe I'll actually have time to watch a couple of TV shows tonight.

I did a flip turn and started back down the lane.

Dinner. What do we have in the kitchen? Some leftover macaroni. I can't remember if we have any chicken in the freezer. Maybe tuna fish sandwiches and salad will do. Just once I'd like a day when I don't have to take care of everything.

I took another breath and saw Sunny, head still bent over his notebook. He works so hard just for the little things. I really don't have the right to complain about my life.

Although Sunny is eighteen and my older brother, I pretty much take care of him because he has Down syndrome. He's a year and a half older than I am, but we're both juniors. His real name is Abraham Walter Johnson. My father began calling him Sunny before his first birthday, because Sunny was always smiling and happy. When I was born, my parents gave me the name Skye to match his nickname.

My dad liked to say that whenever his children were around, he'd have a Sunny Skye. Believe me, there's nothing anyone can say about our names that I haven't already heard. Sometimes I wish Dad had thought about what having these names would mean to us. Sunny never seemed to mind, but my name has always driven me crazy. No one ever spells it right, and half the time people ask me what my *real* name is.

Apparently the Sunny Skye wasn't enough to keep my dad happy, because he left us when I was only five. He sent checks and letters from time to time for the first three years or so, but we haven't heard from him at all in the last seven years.

Sometimes when I start to feel sorry for myself, I look at my mom. Life has been hard on her. Mom has to work two jobs, just to make ends meet. When she can, she puts a little money into savings for my college. She's a secretary in the daytime and tends bar most nights at a restaurant downtown. But she always tries to find time for us. She doesn't always succeed, but knowing she tries means a lot. I don't know how she keeps it all together without going crazy.

Sundays are strictly reserved for family time, because it's the only full day of the week she has off. She gets up early and cleans the house before Sunny and I are even out of bed. Then we all have breakfast together and decide how to spend the rest of the day. She makes a big fuss about spending the whole day with Sunny and me, doing "family" things like going to the zoo or taking a picnic to the park. If she gets any other night off, she'll usually let me go over to a friend's house, but that doesn't happen very often.

Dealing with Sunny's problems isn't easy for either of us. Mom is always worried about his health, because he gets sick so often. I feel like I don't have room to mess up. Mom doesn't need to have any extra worry because of me; Sunny takes up enough of her worry.

Sunny takes up a lot of my worry too. Whenever he's at home, I have to be there, and if I want to go anywhere, he has to go with me. I've argued with Mom about it a lot. I keep telling her that Sunny can handle being home alone for an hour or two without a problem, but she just won't listen. It really bugs me the way she coddles him. I've always said she needs to push him to be more independent. And since last year, his school occupational therapist has told her the same thing. Mom doesn't listen, though. I think she feels bad about not being around much, so she makes up for it the only way she can. I don't know what she's going to do when I leave for college. I intend to find a way to go to college, and I'm not taking him with me.

Everyone else in my lane finished, so I just did an extra fifty. I stopped at the wall.

"You're not done yet," Deb informed me as I took off my goggles.

"Yeah, I know. I'll catch the rest at the end of practice."

"Where were you today?" Hannah asked. We usually met at her locker after school and then walked over to the pool together.

"Jenny wanted to talk to me about something," I said.

"Did she tell you about Mike?" she asked.

"What? How did you know?"

"Everyone's heard. So, are you going out with him?"

"He hasn't even asked me out yet."

"Don't worry, he will," Hannah said. "And no girl in her right mind would turn *him* down."

~

I was late for practice again.

"Where were you?" Deb whispered as I hurried to join the team on deck. Coach looked at me, shook his head, and made a mark on the clipboard.

I ignored Deb's question and concentrated on the stretching. It was hard to believe that two weeks had already gone by since I first found out about Mike.

During warm-up I had trouble settling into my rhythm. I couldn't get my mind off Mike. We had been out three times already, which was some kind of miracle, considering that I had only had two other real dates in my entire lifetime. He said he had almost asked me out once last year, when Jon and Jenny had first gotten together, but I guess DeAnna stepped in about then.

"You stood me up again today," Hannah said as we rested before sets. "It looks like things are heating up between you and Mike."

"He met me at my locker and we got to talking," I said casually.

"So did you get any?" she asked. Hannah enjoys shocking people with her blunt talk.

"What?" I said. I could feel my cheeks getting hot. "We were just talking."

"Uh-huh, sure. I've heard that one before."

Christie and Deb laughed with her.

"Whatever," I said. "As if I had enough time to do more than talk."

"Well, you know if you're quick—" Christie began.

"Ladies," Coach Sullivan cut in, "as soon as you're ready to listen to your first set, let me know."

"We're ready," I said quickly.

Our first set was the biggest one of the evening, and it took us nearly fifty minutes to finish. We were working hard and didn't have time to do much talking. Then when Coach brought kick boards over to our lane, we cheered. Our second set was just light kicking. We paired off, Hannah with me and Christie with Deb, and talked as we kicked.

"So, were you and Mike talking about anything important? You know, anything mushy that would be good gossip?" Hannah asked.

"He wanted me to cut practice."

"Then why are you here?"

I sighed. "Come on, Hannah. You know what this season means to me."

"Skye, he is the hottest guy at school. I can't believe you decided to come here instead of going with him!"

"*You* would have skipped, huh?"

"Oh yeah," she said, nodding her head and grinning mischievously. "In fact, I probably would have asked him to skip with me a long time ago."

"Well, it didn't matter anyway," I said, trying to save face. "Coach Peters busted us in the hall. He sent Mike on to practice, and will probably keep him there an extra hour doing push-ups tonight."

Hannah laughed. "You're going to have to stay for Sullivan too," she reminded me.

I nodded glumly.

"And to think, instead of being worked into the ground, the two of you could have been off in the privacy of his car somewhere."

"Yeah, right, it would have been really private with Sunny in the backseat."

"No, no. You'd put Sunny in the front. You and Mike would be in the back!"

I smacked my hand on top of the water and sent a spray into her face. "You've got a sick mind," I said.

"Oh, and tell me you weren't thinking the same thing," she retorted, splashing back.

"I wasn't!" I felt myself flushing again. I had always listened to the locker room jokes, had even contributed occasionally, but I had never been the object of the jokes before now.

Hannah laughed and shook her head. "If you want to play all innocent with me, fine. Just remember that I know you."

I laughed uncomfortably. Just because I had been dating the cutest guy at school for a couple of weeks, people were already starting to assume that we were sleeping together. If I tried to set the record straight, I'd sound like a complete nerd.

Not only was Mike my first boyfriend, he was also incredibly popular. I still didn't know what he saw in me. I was usually quiet in school and had hardly ever dated before. He was the captain of the football team and had left a string of broken hearts last year. I didn't want to be the next one.

"So, are you and Jenny going to double for homecoming?" Hannah asked.

"I don't know," I said. Inside, I was excited about going to the homecoming dance for the first time, but part of me was afraid Mike and I wouldn't last that long. "What do you think homecoming will be like this year?" I asked Hannah.

She shrugged. "The same as it's been every year. Boring." Hannah was a senior and co-captain of the team. She was ready to graduate and move on with her life. I could tell she didn't love swimming the way she used to; she had burned out. Almost everyone understood that she was on the team this year for one reason: to get her four-year letter in swimming. I wasn't sure if Coach had figured it out, though. He was still pushing her the same way he had since she was a freshman, the same way he pushed all of us.

Hannah was a strong swimmer, but after the first three meets of our season, she was still nearly five seconds off the qualifying time for the state championships in the 200 yard freestyle, and almost nine seconds off in the 500 yard freestyle.

I had my heart set on going to state this year. I was just a second and a half off in the 200, and four seconds in the 500. I had decided before the season started that I was going to state this year if it killed me. It still bugged me that I hadn't made it last year. It was the first time I had set a goal for myself and not made it.

Ever since my freshman year, swimming had been the center of my life. I joined a year-round swim team, forfeiting my allowance to pay the monthly dues. We didn't have team practice on Sundays, but I usually found a way to get to the pool to work out by myself anyway. That summer I had read biographies on Mark Spitz, Summer Sanders, and Rowdy Gaines. I had talked to sports trainers and learned about visualization and relaxation techniques. I was focused and on track. I was hoping to get a swimming scholarship to help pay my way through college.

Our local college didn't have a team, and for me that was both good and bad. It gave me a good reason to get out of town. But going to a college out of town would cost a lot more. Keeping my grades up, making state qual times, and then finding any potential scholarships had been my only goals at the beginning of the school year. But that was before Mike had asked me out.

"Of course," Hannah said slowly, "homecoming will be different in one way. I'm going with Jeremy."

I stopped kicking. "You're what?"

"Going with Jeremy," she said over her shoulder. She hadn't stopped kicking.

I just waited there in the middle of the lane and watched her turn around at the wall and come back to me. When she got close I turned around and pushed off the bottom, kicking alongside her again. "Who's Jeremy? And why are you going with *him?*"

"Jeremy Buck. He's a senior over at East."

"Hannah, you're avoiding the question. Why are you going with him?"

"Lou and I broke up last night."

I groaned. "Not again!"

"This time it's for good."

I looked at her in disbelief. She and Lou had been dating since they were sophomores. They broke up at least four times each year, and each time it was "for good."

"Have you already asked Jeremy to homecoming?"

"Yep." She nodded. "I asked him last night."

"When did you and Lou break up?" We reached the wall and turned together. "Hannah? When exactly did you break up?"

"Around eight," she admitted.

"What did you do, call Jeremy as soon as you got off the phone with Lou?"

"No!" she said.

I looked at her and raised my eyebrows.

"I called Jeremy as soon as Lou left," she mumbled.

"Hannah! I can't believe you did this!"

"What?" she said.

"Homecoming's still a month away!"

"So?"

"So? So what happens when you and Lou get back together, but you've already got a date for homecoming?"

She shook her head. "I told you, we broke up for good."

"This time," I added sarcastically.

"I'm serious!"

"You always are!" I exclaimed. I could tell by the look on her face that this was not the time to push the issue. "Okay, okay. It's for good this time. What happened?"

She shook her head. "I really don't want to talk about it."

"Are you sure?"

She nodded.

"Okay," I said. "So what's Jeremy like?"

She grinned. "He is absolutely fine! Blond hair, blue eyes, a couple of freckles on his cute nose...." She sighed. "Plus he's really nice. I mean, an absolute sweetie."

"And Lou's not?" I asked dryly.

"Well, lately Lou's been taking me for granted." She paused and shook her head again. "I don't want to talk about Lou. What about Mike?"

"What about him?"

"How are things going?"

"Fine," I said. "Even if we don't cut practice together."

She laughed. "I'm sure you find time together other ways. Besides, this is your year to go to state. You don't have time to cut practice."

"Thank you!"

"For what?"

"For saying what I was trying to tell you earlier!"

"I know." She winked. "I told you I know you."

We finished the kick set and put the boards up. The rest of practice consisted of a really difficult set with intervals so fast we didn't have time to talk. I cooled down with the rest of my lane, and then while everyone else got out of the pool, I did a couple of easy laps, waiting for Coach to come tell me what my extra set would be. My stomach grumbled, but I ignored it. Dinner would be late tonight.

Gliding into the wall on the last twenty-five, I rolled over onto my back and did a lazy back flip turn on the wall. I stood up and took off my goggles. Coach was on the side of the pool, busy talking to a couple of freshmen.

Sunny was standing in front of my lane, frowning. "Come on, Skye. We've got to get home!"

"Sunny, just go sit down. I'll let you know when I'm ready to leave."

He put his hands on his hips and frowned even more. His eyebrows were drawn together, and his lower lip was sticking out. "I'm hungry!"

"I don't care! You're not going to starve if you have to wait just a little bit longer. Just go sit down!"

He took a deep breath as if he was going to say something, but then he just pursed his lips and stood there staring at me.

I shook my head. "The longer you stand here and stare at me, the longer I have to stay. So you might as well just go sit down now."

Sunny turned to leave just as Coach came over to my lane. "Hey, Sunny, how are you doing?" Coach asked, smiling.

Sunny continued to pout. "I'm hungry."

Coach nodded. "Me too. Tell you what. I've got a couple of granola bars in my bag over there. Why don't you go get one for each of us?"

Sunny's whole face lit up. "Really?"

"Really."

"Thanks!" He turned to run and get them.

"Sunny!" I yelled. "Walk on the deck!"

He slowed down. I rolled my eyes. He was here with me every day, and yet at least twice a week I had to tell him not to run in the pool area. It drove me crazy.

Coach chuckled before he turned to me. Then his face became stern. "Why were you late again?"

"It's unexcused, Coach."

"Why were you late?"

"I just was."

He looked at me for a long minute. I could tell he was trying to decide whether or not to dig for details. Finally he said, "Skye, you're close to state times. Do you want to go this year?"

I reddened. "You know I do!"

"Then you need to start training like a state swimmer. That means you're here on time." When I tried to interrupt, he continued, "And when you're in the water, you give 100 percent to each set. Even," he said, looking more stern, "during the kick sets."

I looked down at the water.

"I know you're aware of my policy about keeping swimmers after practice if they're late, but I also know that you need to take Sunny home."

I shook my head. "Don't treat me differently because of him. I owe you a sprint set."

Sunny came up, holding two granola bars. "Which one do you want? One's chocolate chip, the other's raisin nut." Sunny wrinkled his nose.

Coach smiled. "I'll take the raisin nut," he said.

"Thanks! Thanks a lot!" Sunny said, beaming. He turned and started to run back to the bleachers. I opened my mouth, but just before I started to yell his name, he slowed down. He looked over his shoulder and gave me a bashful little grin.

"Okay, Skye. Ten one hundreds on the minute-five."

"What?" I squeaked.

"If we're going to get you to state qual times—" he began.

"Yeah, but this is the end of practice!"

"Skye," he warned.

"I'm going, I'm going," I muttered, clearing my goggles and putting them on.

I watched the pace clock till it hit the thirty, and then I took off. I pushed hard and made all ten of them, but just barely. If there had been an eleventh one, I would have missed the interval.

"Nice work today," Coach said. "Be sure you do at least a two hundred easy."

Panting, I nodded. I swam the first hundred nice and slow freestyle, and felt my muscles start to relax. At the hundred I stopped and tossed my goggles and cap up on the deck. I ducked under and sighed in relief as the cool water slid through my hair down to my scalp. For the last hundred I did a mixture of breaststroke, backstroke, and even a twenty-five of sidestroke.

I got out of the pool, picked up my cap and goggles, and waved to Coach as I headed to the locker room. I took a hot shower, rinsed out my suit, and got dressed quickly. I knew that Sunny would be waiting anxiously outside. He'd probably whine all the way home, and then continue to whine until dinner was made. Thinking about it didn't put me in a good mood.

All brothers and sisters argue, but I always felt I had been denied that right. With Sunny, I couldn't really fight, because he couldn't fight back. He was my responsibility, and I had to deal with it. It wasn't always bad, but the problem was that the responsibility never went away. Sunny was always there. I couldn't do anything without him.

When I stepped out into the lobby, Sunny was waiting. He grinned as soon as he saw me, picked up his bag, and started toward the door.

"Ready?"

I sighed and nodded. It was hard staying mad at someone who was usually happy and nice.

CHAPTER TWO

We walked home in silence. It was the end of twilight. With the upcoming time change, I knew I'd finish the swim season walking home in complete darkness. Sometimes it was nice having Sunny with me. Tonight, though, I didn't want to talk.

When we got home, he immediately disappeared into his room. I knew he'd change clothes and then come out to the living room to finish his homework. I dropped my bags in my room and hung my suit up to dry before heading to the kitchen to make dinner.

I had forgotten to take the chicken out of the freezer again. I decided I didn't want to take the time to defrost it so I put it in the fridge to use tomorrow night. I heated up some vegetable soup and made tuna fish sandwiches.

"Okay, Sunny, dinner's ready," I called into the living room. "Come get your drink."

He shuffled into the kitchen. "What is it?"

"Soup and tuna fish."

He made a face. "Again?"

"Hey, any time you want to start cooking gourmet meals, you just go right ahead."

He shook his head and pulled the milk out of the fridge. I grabbed my can of Diet Coke and my food and headed to the living room. On the occasional nights Mom was home, the three of us ate at the table. If it was just Sunny and me, we ate on the couch and watched *Friends* reruns. It was the only time we were allowed to have TV on until all homework was done, including Sunny's. I used to try to watch it other times, but Sunny always forgot and told Mom about some show we had seen. So I found it easier to just follow the rules.

We were halfway through *Friends* when Sunny turned to me. "Skye?"

"What?"

"Why did you have to stay late today?"

"Because I was late getting there."

He was quiet for a minute, then he said, "Why?"

I groaned. "I just was, okay?"

"It was Mike's fault, wasn't it?"

"No, Sunny, it was my fault. Now shut up, would you?"

He subsided for a while. But when the next commercial came on, he got up, stood right in front of me and said, "Skye?"

"What now?"

"Teach me how to thwim." Sometimes Sunny lisped when he was nervous or excited.

I choked on my Diet Coke. He tried to pat me on the back. I pushed him away. "No. Uh-uh. No way," I said when I recovered my breath.

"Why not?"

"Because, Sunny, you may not remember your last swim lesson, but I do."

"I've never had swim lessons."

"Oh, yes you have! You and I had our first lesson together." I shook my head, remembering.

Dad had taken us to the recreation center and dropped us off. He was supposed to stick around, but for some reason he didn't. Sunny started screaming as soon as his foot hit the water. At first the instructor tried to coax him in, but then he decided that maybe Sunny would stop yelling once he was all the way in, so he lifted him into the water. By the time he got Sunny back out of the pool, all of the kids in the class were screaming, one had a bloody nose where Sunny had elbowed him, and the instructor was bleeding where Sunny had bit him. Disaster doesn't even begin to describe it.

Mom was called in from work to pick us up. She and Dad had a terrific fight about it that night. They had fought ever since I could remember, but it had gotten really bad around that time. Not too long after that he left for good.

"I never had swim lessons," Sunny repeated stubbornly.

"Yes, you did!" I said again. "When you were seven."

"That was a long time ago," he said, calming down. "I want to learn how to swim."

"Why?" I asked.

He shrugged. "I have fun when I go with you to the pool on Sundays."

"That's not swimming," I said. "That's just splashing around."

"I know. That's why I want to learn."

"Well, I'm not going to teach you," I said, picking up my plate and glass. I headed into the kitchen. He followed me.

"Why not?"

"Because, Sunny, as soon as you think something's hard, you quit."

"I do not!"

"Yes, you do! Remember soccer? And baseball?"

He frowned at me. "Mom made me do those. I didn't want to."

"You still quit."

"I didn't like soccer or baseball. I'll like swimming."

"I'm not going to teach you," I repeated.

"Why not?" he demanded again.

"Because I said so!" I yelled.

"That's not a reason." He pouted.

"Yeah, well, it's the only one you're going to get!" I said. I closed my eyes and counted to ten.

"You're not being fair!" he shouted at me.

"Yeah, like it's real fair that I have to be chained to you all the time," I muttered.

He looked at me for a minute, then turned and stomped into the living room. He picked up all his books, stomped as loudly as he could to his room, and slammed the door.

Great, I said to myself. *Just great. He'll go blabbing to Mom about me being mean again.* I sighed and began putting the dishes in the dishwasher.

The doorbell rang. I wiped my hands on the towel and flipped on the porch light. I looked through the peephole, then I unlocked the door. It was Mike. I started grinning. For some reason I felt warm all over. Maybe the evening wasn't a complete loss after all.

"Hey," I said, opening the door. "What's up?"

He shrugged. "I was just in the area and thought I'd drop by."

"Are you just now getting home from practice?"

He nodded.

I stared. "Seriously? What did you have to do?"

"Coach decided to make an example of me." He sighed. "Not only did I have to do the 150 push-ups for being six minutes late, I also had to run six laps for being six minutes late."

"I'm sorry," I said.

"Me too. But if you invite me in, I bet you can make me feel better," he said with a grin.

I hesitated, and before I could answer, Sunny spoke up from behind me. "We aren't supposed to have friends over at night, Skye." He was glaring at Mike.

"I know that, Sunny!" I yelled at him. "Why don't you just go sulk in your room some more?"

I heard him stomp back down the hall and slam his door again.

I turned back to Mike. "I'm sorry. Sometimes I can get him to cover for me, but tonight's a bad night. He's mad at me anyway."

"Okay. If I can't come in, why don't you come out? We can just sit in my car and talk for a little while."

I thought about it briefly, but I knew he wanted to do more than just talk. His kisses left me all tingly, but they also scared me a little. I was constantly afraid of doing something stupid. Where exactly was your tongue supposed to go anyway?

"Not tonight, Mike," I said. "Sunny's so mad I don't know what he might pull. I'm sorry."

"It's okay," he said. He started backing down the steps. I could tell he was disappointed.

"Hey," I said, clearing my throat and feeling awkward. "You're going to leave without a good-night kiss?"

He smiled and came back. We kissed for a few minutes. During the second kiss, his hand strayed up my side and I broke the embrace. "I've got to go."

"Yeah. Sure. Me too." He turned and jogged out to his car.

"See you tomorrow?" I called, just as his door shut. He honked as he pulled away.

I went back inside and finished putting the dishes and leftovers away. I took my frustrations out on the cabinets, slamming the doors every chance I got.

I had known who Mike Banner was for the last three years. There wasn't a girl in school who didn't know who he was. But before last month, I hadn't exchanged more than ten words with him. I couldn't believe it when he actually asked for my phone number. There are a lot of times I still can't believe it.

It was a good thing Sunny was hiding in his room. I could have killed him with a smile on my face. Sometimes he's not so bad, but nights like tonight really made me wish I was an only child. I was getting that feeling more and more lately, it seemed. I was feeling suffocated even though it was the same pattern and routine we had had for years.

Of course, if Mom and Dad had been like most parents, they wouldn't have tried to have another kid after having Sunny. They still don't know what causes Down syndrome, so most couples who have a Down's kid decide not to have any more. The one time I tried to ask Mom about it, she quickly changed the conversation.

Sunny and I share our mom's blond hair, but other than that, we don't look much alike. I know a lot of that has to do with the Down syndrome. His face is all round and soft, like a baby's.

We don't act much alike either. I'm usually on a pretty even keel, and it takes a lot to get me upset. Sunny's either really happy or really upset; there's no middle ground. But even though he gets upset quickly and a lot, he doesn't hold grudges for very long.

Even our interests are different. He likes sci-fi stuff, and fantasy. It took us a couple of years to convince him that he'd never find a magician who could fix him. He's never cared about swimming. Until now.

I went down the hall to my room, which was across from Sunny's. I turned my stereo up and flopped on my bed. For a long while I just lay there, staring at the ceiling and listening to the music.

Finally I got up and went to my desk. I breezed through my homework in forty-five minutes. Then I called Jenny, and we just talked for another half hour. Well, mostly I talked and she just listened. That's one of my favorite things about her: even though she loves to talk, she's always ready to listen. I told her all about my latest problem with Sunny, and then told her about Mike coming over.

"Too bad Sunny was in a bad mood," she said sympathetically. "You could have invited Mike in and had some fun tonight." She was joking the way we always did, but I just wasn't in the mood. I thought about her comment. "Even if Sunny wasn't being a snot," I said, "I'm not sure I could have had Mike come in."

"Why not?"

"Well, Sunny has a hard enough time keeping his mouth shut. And if Mike had put his hands on me, even for just a hug, I know Sunny would have blabbed."

"What do you mean?"

"I can tell Sunny doesn't like Mike."

"Really?"

"Yeah."

"You sure he's not just jealous? You know, upset that you want to spend time with Mike and not with him?"

"Well, he likes you, even though I spend a lot of time with you. No," I said, "he just doesn't like Mike."

"I wonder why?" Jenny said.

"I have no idea."

"You're really a saint to put up with Sunny the way you do," Jenny said. "I think I'd go crazy."

I felt a twinge of guilt. "No, I'm not a saint. I just put up with him. A saint would put up with him and be nice about it."

"You are nice to him—" Jenny began.

"No, I'm not," I said. I could feel my throat tightening up. "Look, Jen, I gotta take off. I'll see you tomorrow."

"Don't forget to come early."

"I won't. Later."

"See ya."

We hung up. I lay back on my bed and the tears rolled silently down my cheeks, then dripped into my ears with an annoying tickle. *I should be nicer to Sunny,* I thought. *I should treat him better than I do. But things just aren't the same anymore. I promise myself I'll be nice to him, and then he does something stupid that makes me get frustrated with him all over again. I keep trying to raise my level of patience, but lately it just seems to keep slipping lower.*

Resolutely I wiped my face dry and got up. I went to the kitchen and made two cups of hot chocolate. I took them back to his room and kicked as gently as I could on the bottom of his door.

"Go away!" he said.

"Come on, Sunny, I've got hot cocoa."

"I don't care!"

I sighed and tried to stay calm. "Come on, open up. My hands are full."

"I don't want any."

"We need to go over your Western Civ," I said.

"I already did!"

I clenched my teeth to keep from screaming. I couldn't do anything right. "Fine." I turned around and went back to the kitchen, where I dumped his cocoa down the drain. Then I turned on the TV to wait for Mom.

After a while I had calmed down enough to go back to Sunny's room and try again, but his light was off so I didn't bother knocking. Mom came home about an hour later.

"Hi, honey. How was your day?"

"Fine," I said. "How was yours?"

"Ugh," she said, kicking off her shoes. "It was okay. The office is nice and slow with Mr. Barnes gone, but he comes back day after tomorrow, and I know he'll have a lot for me to catch up on. And the bar was slow tonight, so they let me go early. Not much for tips."

"I'm sorry," I said, following her into the kitchen.

"Anything new going on in school?" she asked.

"No. Same boring stuff."

She laughed. "As long as boring means you're getting A's in everything, I guess that's okay." She paused as she scanned the contents of the fridge. "How's your boyfriend? Mark?"

"Mike," I said automatically. She could never remember my friends' names. "He's fine."

"I'd like to meet him sometime," she said as she pulled out some lettuce and the last tomato for a salad.

I nodded, but knew it wouldn't happen. She just wasn't ever home long enough to meet many of my friends. Jenny was the only one of my friends she really knew. "Hey, did you get Thursday off?" It would be our first home meet of the season.

"I'm sorry," she said. She didn't need to say anything else, so she didn't.

"It's okay."

"Where's Sunny?"

"He went to bed early tonight."

She frowned. "Is he feeling okay?"

I shrugged. "He didn't say anything to me."

She looked at me for a minute. "Are *you* feeling okay? You look a little flushed." She leaned forward. "Your eyes are red. Have you been crying?"

I pulled back from her. "I'm fine. I'm just a little tired. We have a student council meeting before school tomorrow. I should probably go to bed now."

"Skye, is there something we should talk about?"

"No, Mom. I'm fine."

"You sure you're okay?"

"Yeah. I'm fine." I turned and started down the hall. "Good night, Mom."

"Good night, honey. Sleep well."

"You too."

I got ready for bed, turned out the light, and crawled under the covers. I tossed and turned for about fifteen minutes before I decided that my headache wasn't going to let me sleep. I needed some ibuprofen. I got up again and opened my bedroom door.

Sunny was creeping out of his room. He jumped when he saw me.

"What do you need?" I whispered.

"Nothing," he said.

"What's wrong?"

"Nothing," he said again.

"Well, then, go back to bed."

"No. I want to talk to Mom."

"Sunny, she's had a long day. Just let it wait for tomorrow."

"No!"

"Then tell me what's wrong. I'll help you."

"I want to talk to Mom!" he shouted.

"Shhh!"

"Leave me alone!" he continued to shout. "You don't really want to help me anyway!" He turned and ran down the hall to Mom's room.

I sighed. My head was throbbing. I went into the bathroom, took some ibuprofen, and went back to bed. I was still awake two hours later.

∽

The next morning, I pulled myself out of bed the instant the alarm went off. Usually I hit the snooze three or four times. Today, though, I knew I had to get up early, in spite of the fact that I had had hardly any sleep and my eyes were puffy and swollen.

On my way to the shower, I stuck my head in Sunny's door and flipped on his light. "We're leaving early this morning. I have a meeting."

He burrowed further under his blankets.

"I'm serious, Sunny. We're leaving at seven."

I left his light on and headed to the bathroom. The shower made me feel better. I dried my hair almost all of the way, leaving it just a little damp so it wouldn't get all staticky. I used more makeup than usual, trying to disguise the death-warmed-over look. I did one last check in the mirror. Yep, I looked almost normal. No one would be able to tell anything was wrong.

When I came out, Sunny was waiting at the door for his turn in the bathroom. He went in without saying anything to me, and he still wasn't smiling. I knew he must be really mad at me. Usually he was so happy and hyper in the mornings it was downright disgusting.

I got dressed and went to the kitchen. There was a note taped to the fridge with my name on it.

> Skye—
> Sunny says he'd like to learn how to swim. I think it would be wonderful physical therapy for him. I also know how much you enjoy swimming and spending time in the pool. I would like to hire you as Sunny's private instructor. I can't pay you as much as instructors normally charge, but I will be able to pay you. We can talk more tonight.
>   Love,
>   Mom
> P.S. Why were you late to practice yesterday?

I had to read through the note twice. After the second time, I crumpled it up into a ball.

I heard the bathroom door open. "*Sunny!*" I exploded. "Get your butt in here!"

He came down the hall slowly, still wearing his bathrobe.

"How dare you? How dare you go to Mom about swimming lessons when I already said no!" I shouted.

"Because—" he started.

"No!" I cut him off. "There's no excuse for this! I told you no, and like a spoiled brat you went running to Mother! I am so sick of you always getting your way, of you acting like we have to do everything for you! Tonight," I said, heading toward him, "tonight when Mom gets home, you are going to tell her you changed your mind and you're never going to bring up swimming lessons again, is that clear?"

By this time he was backing up rapidly, and tears were rolling down his chubby cheeks. "I want to learn how to thwim!" he cried.

"And I want a life doing something besides baby-sitting you!" I cried back. "I want a brother who doesn't go tattling to Mom whenever I do the tiniest thing wrong. We can't all get what we want!"

"I hate you!" he cried, slamming his door.

"I don't care!" I yelled back at his door.

I stormed back to the kitchen, but I was way too upset to eat anything. Just thinking of the note made me seethe. I couldn't sit still. I paced back and forth in the kitchen for the next ten minutes.

With a start I looked at the clock and saw it was seven. I strode down the hall and pounded on Sunny's door.

"Let's go. Now!" I said into the door.

He didn't respond.

"Sunny, don't make me count to three," I warned. Still no answer. I started counting, "One...two..."

His door opened. His face was all splotchy and there were still tears sneaking out of his eyes. His hair hadn't been combed and his shirt was untucked.

I jerked my head toward the front door. "Let's go. You're not going to make me late on top of all this."

Sniffling, he picked up his backpack and walked to the front door.

"For Pete's sake, tuck your shirt in," I said as we walked out the door. "And you better stop crying before we reach the corner."

We walked in silence again, him trailing me by about ten feet. We got to the school and walked inside. I started up the stairs to go to my locker, and then stopped to turn and look at him. He had already disappeared into the hallway, just the way he was supposed to. I turned and continued on to my locker and then to the student council meeting.

CHAPTER
THREE

The day was long and slow, and I had a hard time concentrating on classes. I was still mad at Sunny. I knew I wouldn't see him till school got out, because most of his classes were self-contained. For PE, Art, and Civics, he got to be with other juniors, but thankfully I wasn't in any of those classes.

I was also looking for Mike, hoping to find out if he was mad about last night. But I didn't see him all day, which wasn't exactly unusual. Sometimes we ran into each other, but not always. He knew where to find me between classes, and I knew what times he would be at his locker. Today, I didn't even pass him in the halls, and I was afraid to go looking for him. *Play it cool,* I thought. *Maybe nothing is wrong.*

When the last bell rang, I met Jenny out in the hall again. She looked lost in thought.

"You okay?" I asked.

"Huh?" She looked at me.

"You've been awfully quiet all day. Something wrong?"

"No," she said, shaking her head.

We were separated for a minute in the hallway by a crowd of people, but then we came back together. When we turned down our hall, we passed DeAnna, Mike's ex-girlfriend. I smiled tentatively, but she looked right through me.

Jenny and I made our way to our lockers and began pulling our books out in silence. I knew something was wrong. Jenny was always talking.

"Jenny, what's wrong?" I repeated.

"It was our four-month anniversary yesterday, but Jon didn't call last night."

We stepped apart. A tear slipped out of the corner of her eye.

"And?"

"And I haven't seen him all day."

I thought quickly. "He had a dentist's appointment yesterday, right?"

"Yeah."

"Maybe he couldn't talk. You know, because he had novocaine or something."

She just looked at me and gave me half a smile. "You are always calm, cool, and collected," she said.

"Me?" I laughed. "You got the wrong girl. I haven't seen Mike either," I said, and suddenly I was on the brink of tears myself.

"Oh no!" Jenny cried. I reached out to hug her.

"Hey, now, that's my job!" a voice said beside me. We broke the hug, and there was Jon, grinning. His grin faded when he saw the tears. "What's wrong?" he asked.

"Nothing," Jenny and I said simultaneously, and we started to laugh. Laughing right after crying was so stupid, we started laughing even harder. We couldn't stop. Jon watched us with a puzzled grin for a few seconds, then he finally started to laugh too.

Jenny reached up, put her arms around his neck, and gave him a kiss.

I glanced over my shoulder, looking for Mike. The hallway was empty. I sighed and picked up my backpack.

"Skye? Are you going to be okay?" Jenny asked, looking at me over Jon's shoulder.

I grinned. "I'll be fine."

Jenny looked at Jon. "Have you seen Mike?"

He shook his head. "Not since third hour."

"I'm sure nothing's wrong," Jenny said to me.

"Yeah," I said. "He probably just didn't want to be late to practice again."

"That's it," she said, agreeing instantly.

Jon tugged on her hand. "Come on, let's get going before we're late."

"Yeah," I said, shutting my locker. "I've got to go meet Hannah. Have fun at gymnastics practice."

"I'll call you tonight," Jenny called after me as I walked down the hall. I waved as I turned the corner.

When I got to Hannah's locker, she was just slamming it shut. She looked at me in surprise. "I didn't expect to see you here," she said.

"Why not?"

"You know." She grinned. "I thought maybe you and Mike were going to skip today for real."

"Nope," I said, shaking my head. "Let's go."

Together we walked past the tennis courts to the community center. I listened to Hannah ramble. She was so wrapped up in talking about Jeremy that she didn't notice how quiet I was. I didn't say more than three words the whole time.

We walked into the lobby. "Hey, Gail!" I said to the pool manager.

"See you on deck," Hannah said, heading directly into the locker room. I stayed to talk to Gail.

"Hey, Skye! How are you doing?" She was seated behind the front desk, going through some papers.

"Fine," I said. "I thought Tuesday was your day off."

"It's supposed to be," she sighed. "But the next session of lessons starts next week, and I've got to get a lot of paperwork done. It's a lot easier to do here than at home."

"Oh," I said. "Who's working tonight?"

She arched an eyebrow at me. "You know my guards' schedules as well as I do," she said. "Sometimes I think you know their schedules better than they do!"

I laughed. Being around the pool every day had put me on a friendly basis with all of the lifeguards as well as with Gail. I loved to just sit around and chat with them. Most of the guards were working their way through the college in our town, and several of them had graduated from our school in the last couple of years. About half the team knew the guards as well as I did, the other half kind of ignored them, like Hannah did.

"I've got a lifeguard training class coming up in January," Gail said. "Are you going to take it and then come work for me this summer?"

"I don't know," I said. "I mean, I'd love to, but I don't know if Mom would let me. You know, I've got to watch Sunny and stuff."

"When he came in a few minutes ago, he didn't look too happy."

"I'm sure he's not. I yelled at him this morning."

"So," she said, putting the papers to one side. "Are you still dating that guy?"

"Mike." I nodded.

She whistled. "How long have you been dating now?"

"A couple of weeks."

"Dating for two whole weeks! It must be love!"

"Gail! Not even!"

She laughed. "Bring on the wedding bells!"

My face was on fire. I could feel it. I had never really had a boyfriend before. I had gone out on a few dates, but I had never had a relationship. This thing with Mike was different. I had never had a guy pay this much attention to me. He left notes in my locker and called almost every night. One day he had even brought me a rose.

Mike was the quarterback of the football team, he was cute, he was popular, and he drove a great car. Heads turned when we walked down the hall together, and I loved it. But I knew that was different from loving him.

"Oops, you better get moving," she said, glancing out the window. "Coach just pulled into the parking lot."

"Thanks," I said, heading to the locker room. "Will you be around when practice is over?"

"I hope not," she said, picking up the next stack of papers.

I laughed. "See ya later."

She waved and I headed into the locker room.

~

The rest of the night was pretty miserable. It felt like Coach was trying to kill us all that afternoon. I kind of expected it, since it was early in the season and we had a meet coming up on Thursday. Usually I enjoyed a hard practice, but today it seemed like torture.

My whole lane was quiet. We were all too tired and out of breath to do any talking, even between the sets. Complaining is usually my best event, but after Coach gave me that speech about practicing like a state swimmer last night, I knew I should keep my mouth shut.

After practice, Sunny and I walked home again. He was still sulking, so he answered my questions with a yes or no. After two or three questions, I quit trying. I made fried chicken for dinner, with macaroni on the side.

When Sunny saw the macaroni, he started to make a face, but I glared at him, so he didn't say anything. We ate in silence. As soon as he was done with dinner, he retreated to his room again. I took my homework out to the living room, and worked on it while watching TV. I didn't get much of my homework done.

Three times I picked up the phone to call Mike. The first time, I hung up before I did anything, the second time I hung up after dialing the first four numbers, and the third time I hung up just as it started to ring. I wanted desperately to talk to him, but I wanted *him* to call *me*.

Finally, I called Jenny instead. We only talked for a few minutes. She was expecting Jon to come over, and I didn't want to tie up the phone line anyway, in case Mike was trying to call.

An hour later, though, I was starting to go crazy, so I called her back. Jon had just left. I could tell by the tone of her voice that she was all smiles.

"He didn't say anything about Mike, did he?"

"Noooo, not really."

"What's that mean?"

Jenny sighed. "He just said that Mike was in a bad mood at practice today and wouldn't talk to anybody."

"Even Jon?"

"Especially Jon."

"And," Jenny said tentatively, "he was late for practice again."

I began to feel nauseous. Obviously he hadn't been late because of me.

"Maybe he got a bad grade on that Shakespeare test and stayed to get some help," Jenny suggested. "You know how Mike is about his grade in

English. He's still paranoid about staying eligible for the season," she added.

"I don't know," I said. "I just.... Oh, Jenny, what should I do?"

"Skye, you don't do anything yet. You don't even know for sure if anything's wrong. Just relax a little. You're getting too uptight. You sound just like I did earlier, all upset over nothing."

"Thanks," I said flatly.

"No, I didn't mean—"

"I know what you meant. Thanks a lot."

"I didn't mean it like that, Skye. See, you're just upset right now, and you're taking it out on everyone else."

"I gotta go," I said.

"Skye, call me if you need anything."

I hung up without saying good-bye. Like I needed to hear my best friend say I was uptight. I curled up on the couch and stared at the TV screen. Why didn't Mike call? I went into the kitchen and got myself a Diet Coke from the fridge. I went back into the living room and plopped down on the couch. Then I got back up and walked down the hall.

"Sunny? You done with your homework?" He didn't answer. I opened the door to his room. He was sitting on his bed, reading an R. L. Stine book.

"You're not supposed to come in unless I say you can," he said.

"If you don't answer, I have to come in to make sure you're okay," I retorted. "Where's your homework?"

"I'm done."

"No, you're not."

"Yes, I am!"

I shook my head. "You have a test on Friday. There's no way you could have done all your homework *and* studied for an hour."

He set his jaw in a stubborn line. "I'm done for tonight."

I snatched his book out of his hand. "The week you have a test, you're supposed to study every night for an hour."

He tried to grab his book back, but I easily kept it out of reach.

"Skye, it's only Tuesday. I'll study for an hour tomorrow."

"No good. You have to study every night."

"I did!"

"No, you didn't."

"I did too!" He was shouting now, but I could also tell he was close to tears.

"For an hour?" I put all the doubt I could into my voice.

"Almost."

"How long?"

He looked down and mumbled something.

"What? Speak up!"

"Fifteen minutes."

"Fine," I said, nodding toward his backpack. "You get out your Western Civ book, study, and in forty-five minutes, you can have this book back."

I turned around and pulled the door shut behind me. I stayed just outside his door, to listen to what he was going to do. I didn't hear anything.

The phone rang. My heart jumped into my throat. I forced myself to walk down the hall to the living room phone. There was no reason to run. After all, it could be practically anybody. It could even just be a wrong number, or a telephone sales pitch. I picked it up right before the third ring.

"Hello?" I hoped the person on the other end couldn't hear my heart pounding in my ears.

"Skye?"

"Hi, Mike," I said, grinning enormously. I couldn't help it. His voice just affected me that way. It made me feel warm and happy. I tried to remember what he was wearing the last time I saw him. I had no trouble picturing him relaxing on a couch, wearing his favorite Bull's jersey.

"How are you?"

"Okay," I said carefully. "I didn't see you today."

"Yeah, I know. I missed you."

We were both quiet for a few uncomfortable moments. *Say something,* I thought frantically. *Don't just sit here like an idiot.*

"Hey," I said finally. "Are you coming to our meet on Thursday?"

"Where is it?"

"Home."

"Yeah, I'll be there. I'll be a little late because of practice, but I'll be there."

"Great," I said.

"Look, I've got a ton of homework to do tonight. I'll see you tomorrow."

"Promise?" I teased.

"Promise."

"Bye."

"Bye."

I hung up the phone. I was still smiling. It was okay. He hadn't said much, but he wasn't mad at me. He wasn't avoiding me. Everything was okay.

I picked up the phone to call Jenny and apologize, but hung up halfway through dialing. Her parents didn't like it if she got calls after nine o'clock, and it was already nine thirty.

I watched TV for the next half hour. Then I got up to take Sunny his book. His bedroom light was off. I left his book propped up against the door and went back to the living room.

Mom came home about thirty minutes later. I stayed in the living room while she fixed herself something to eat. She brought her plate out and sat down on the couch next to me.

"Where's Sunny?"

"Sleeping."

"Again? Are you two still fighting?"

I didn't answer. She sighed and put her plate on the table. "Okay. What's wrong?" When I just stared at the TV instead of answering, she got up and turned it off. "Come on, Skye. Talk to your mother."

"I just had a bad day, that's all."

"You're acting like your day was so bad you're planning to go to your own funeral tomorrow. What happened?"

I shrugged. "Really, it's nothing important."

"Okay," she said, imitating my shrug. She picked up her plate again. "When are you going to start teaching Sunny how to swim?"

"Mom, I think he changed his mind."

She looked surprised. "Oh?"

"Yeah. He thought about it and decided he doesn't want lessons."

"Why not?"

I couldn't think of a good reason, so I just shrugged again.

"Think carefully before you answer this, Skye. Has he changed his mind, or are you changing it for him?"

I didn't say anything.

"Because last night, all he could talk about was learning how to swim." She paused. "He really wants you to teach him."

"Mom," I said, groaning. "I don't think it's a good idea."

"Why not?" she asked, setting her plate down and leaning forward.

"Don't you remember his last swimming lesson?"

She looked at me for a minute, her face blank.

"The one he and I took together?" I prompted.

Suddenly she laughed. "That one? Oh, God, Skye, that was years ago!"

"So?"

"So? So Sunny was only, what, six years old?"

"Seven."

"Okay, so he was seven years old. That was almost twelve years ago."

"It was a disaster—" I began.

"Skye." Mom cut me off in her don't-give-me-any-crap tone of voice. "You know that Sunny has grown up a lot since then, just like you have. He didn't know what was going on that day. He was scared and alone and confused. Now he's asking you to teach him how to swim. He knows how much you love swimming, and he's interested in trying it. Give him a chance."

I kept staring at the blank television.

"He wants to be like you, Skye. It's a compliment."

"I don't care. It's bad enough I have to baby-sit him and take him with me all the time. Now you're going to make me teach him how to swim too?"

"Honey, I know you spend a lot of time with him—and I really appreciate it. I have no idea what I'd do if you weren't such a good kid. But he really wants this and it would be so good for him."

"He *always* gets what he wants! What about me? I want some time to do stuff with my friends. And I *really* want that!"

She sighed. "I know, I know. But I want you to teach him too. You know his strengths and limitations, and you can tell if he's getting too tired too quickly. I'll do the best I can. I'll let you go do stuff with your friends on Sundays until three. After all, I want a little time with you too!"

"I don't see why you think he should start swimming," I whined. "It's not like he'd ever be able to be any good at it."

She glared at me. "Skye!"

"What? It's true. He doesn't have the coordination."

"Have you stopped to consider that this will be excellent physical therapy for him? That it will help him build muscles and increase his coordination?"

I bit my lip. I knew it was true. But we had tried without success to get him involved in other activities. I just didn't want to spend any more of my time struggling with him.

"And you'll never know if he'll be any good at it or not if you don't give him the chance. He'll probably have a hard time with it in the beginning," she said, "but so did you. I remember when you were ten and the slowest one in your age group. You wanted to quit, remember?" She stopped to give me a chance to respond. When I didn't answer, she went on. "Everything takes practice. He may be pretty good someday. You've got a natural gift in the water. Why can't he have it, too? You're both my children; you've got the same blood."

I stayed quiet.

"Look, Skye, you've been talking about taking the lifeguard training and getting a part-time job. I'll *pay* you to teach Sunny."

I looked at her and shook my head. "You couldn't afford it."

She arched an eyebrow at me, a trick I envied and had never been able to do. "Oh, really?"

"Really. Do you know how much instructors get for a half-hour private lesson?"

"Do you?" she countered.

I nodded. "The guards at the pool fight over private lessons, because they get between ten and fifteen dollars per half hour."

She hesitated. "Are you sure it's not per hour?"

"Positive."

She looked at me, weighing the issues. "Well," she said slowly, "you're not certified, so you shouldn't earn as much."

"If I'm not certified, I shouldn't be teaching," I said quickly.

"You've got enough years of swimming experience. You can teach. And you're family, so you should give us a discount."

"Mom," I moaned.

She looked at me for a few moments. "I'll give you twenty dollars a week to teach him."

"In addition to my ten dollar allowance?" I asked.

She winced, but nodded.

"How many lessons a week?" I asked. She wasn't going to let me get out of this, so I might as well bargain for the best deal I could get.

"Four lessons a week."

"Four?" I squeaked. "No way. That's too much time. Two."

"That's not enough time. He'll need practice. Four half-hour lessons in a week isn't that much time."

"No more than three," I said stubbornly.

"Okay," she said, "Three lessons a week for fifteen dollars."

"Uh-uh," I said, shaking my head. "Three a week for twenty."

"Three a week for ten," she said. "And I'll let you have the car for the days that you teach him."

I stopped. This one I had to think about. I had craved access to the car ever since getting my license almost six months ago. So far, I had only been allowed to take the car out without Mom on four memorable occasions. If I could have it three times a week! Even if I had to take Sunny with me, it would be better than having to walk to school or bum rides off my friends.

"Three a week for fifteen and the car," I bargained.

She looked at me. "You can either have the car for all three days and ten dollars a week, or you can have the car for two days and fifteen a week. Final offer."

I chewed on my bottom lip while I thought about it. "Three lessons a week, ten dollars, and the car for the lesson days," I said finally. Even though it was a beat-up old Honda, having the car was worth more than five dollars.

"Deal," she said, holding out her hand. We shook on it, and then she picked up her plate and leaned back into the couch.

"I still get time on Sundays to go out with my friends, right?"

She took a deep breath. "Until three o'clock, if you still want it. But any time you want to spend Sunday with your dear old Mom...."

I groaned. "Please, no more guilt trips tonight! I can't handle it!"

After a few minutes, Mom asked, "So what days am I going to have to take the bus to work?"

"Tuesday, Thursday, and Saturday."

"I was hoping it would be a Monday, Wednesday, Friday kind of thing."

I shook my head.

"Aren't most of your meets on Tuesdays and Thursdays?"

"Yeah, so I won't mind spending an extra half hour in the water with him. If I do it after practice, I'll be in the water for a solid three hours at a time."

"I guess that makes sense. Okay. Can we start next week?"

"Yeah." I stood up and stretched. It was time for me to go to bed. "Oh, by the way, Mom, can I get this week's allowance?"

She nodded. "There should be a ten in my purse."

"Okay. See you tomorrow."

"Good night, Skye. Sleep well."

"You too."

I stopped in the kitchen and picked up the ten from Mom's purse. I went to my room and looked in the drawer where I keep my money. Since I didn't have enough time for a job, I rarely had very much cash left over at the end of the week. Tonight I only had seven dollars. I sighed and put it with the ten on my dresser so I could take it with me tomorrow.

I had a hard time getting to sleep. My stomach was tied up in knots and my mind was racing. I had never disobeyed my mother before, but in spite of what I had said to Mom, there was no way I was going to teach Sunny to swim. As it was, I hardly ever had any time to myself. Sunday mornings were going to be nice, but I needed more time of my own. How was I supposed to have a boyfriend if I could never see him? I was going to go crazy if I didn't catch a break. I finally drifted off, thinking about what I was going to do tomorrow.

⁓

The next day at school, I tried to find Mike. But by the time fifth hour rolled around, I knew I couldn't count on seeing him before school got out. So during American Lit I wrote him a note telling him I couldn't meet him after school and gave the note to Jenny, asking her to get it to Jon and to make sure Jon got it to Mike before school let out. Then I told her I was going to try to cut out of physics early and be at the pool as soon as possible. I told her not to wait for me.

She raised her eyebrows. "Jeez, Skye, you're running around like you're a spy or something. What's up?"

"I'll call you tonight and let you know. I don't want to talk about it, in case it doesn't work out."

"Okay." She shrugged. "Whatever."

Luck was with me. Ms. Jenkins had a substitute who really didn't want to be at school any more than the rest of us did. He told us at the beginning of class that if we sat absolutely quiet and just did the work, he'd let us out five minutes early. You could hardly tell anyone was breathing. We were that quiet.

Even with the five-minute head start, I still flew to my locker, threw my books into my pack, and dashed out the door as quickly as I could without looking like a loser.

I walked into the pool lobby just as the rest of school was getting out. Gail looked up from her desk. "You're early."

"I know." I tried to catch my breath. It was amazing. I was in perfect condition in the pool, but put me outside to run, and I ended up panting like a dog within five minutes. "I need to ask a favor."

"No promises, but you can ask."

"The next session of group lessons starts Tuesday, right?"

"Yeah."

"And you have Saturday morning lessons too?"

"Uh-huh." She nodded.

"And the session goes for six weeks?"

"Yeah." She looked at me funny. "I know you know this. Why are you asking?"

"Sunny wants to take some lessons," I said, ignoring the doubt and guilt that had kept me up most of the night. If Sunny wanted to learn how to swim, fine. But I wasn't going to be his teacher. I didn't want to spend any more time with him than I already had to.

She grinned. "Sure. No problem. I don't think that even counts as a favor." She began pulling out the registration forms.

"I haven't gotten to the favor yet."

She stopped and looked at me.

"It's thirty dollars for the Tuesday and Thursday lessons, right?"

"Yeah, and the Saturday lessons are twenty."

"So that's fifty dollars for both of them."

"Glad they still teach addition," she said dryly.

I reached into my pocket. "All I can pay today is fifteen dollars," I said. I decided to keep the extra two for some reason. I wasn't sure what I could do with just two dollars, but I hated not having any cash at all.

I put the money on the desk. "I can pay fifteen a week for the next two weeks, and the last five the week after that."

She looked at me for a long minute.

"Please," I begged. "You know where to find me. I'm here all the time. It's not like I'm going to skip out on you or anything."

"Okay," she said finally. "We can work that out. I have to put it in writing, though," she added.

"That's fine, no problem." I was so relieved I didn't care.

She handed me the registration card. "Here. Fill it out, take it home to have your mom sign it, and bring it back tomorrow."

I hadn't known I'd need Mom's signature for this. "Why does my mom have to sign it?"

"It's the law. To register a minor for a class, we have to have a parent's permission."

"Sunny's eighteen. Can't he just sign for himself?"

"Under normal circumstances, sure. But this is me covering my own backside. Since he's a special ed student and he's still in high school, I need parent permission."

"I can't get my mom to sign this," I began.

"Why not?" she asked suspiciously.

"Because…it's a surprise for her," I said suddenly. The guilt was threatening to come back. I shoved it away. Sunny wanted to learn to swim. Mom wanted him to learn how to swim. I wanted some time of my own. I was doing the best thing. This way, everyone would be happy.

Gail frowned. "What do you mean?"

"Sunny wants to learn how to swim and surprise her with it."

Gail was wavering. I could see it. I made the final push. "Come on, help us out. He wants to do it for her birthday."

"I don't know, Skye," she sighed. "What if something happens? That's why we need the signatures, for liability."

"Yeah, but he's eighteen. He and I will both sign it. You won't be liable for anything."

She started to shake her head.

"Please, Gail. I'm begging here."

"Oh, all right. You both sign it."

"Thanks, Gail. I owe you one."

"You owe me more than that!" she retorted. "Don't forget you still owe me thirty-five dollars."

"I won't," I promised.

The first couple of girls from the team arrived. I stuck around out front until Hannah came in.

"Hey, girl! Thanks for waiting!" she said sarcastically as she came through the door.

"Sorry," I said, waving good-bye to Gail and then following Hannah into the locker room.

"That's twice this week you've ditched me. I'm beginning to think you don't love me anymore."

I laughed. "You know you're the only one for me," I said.

"Yeah, well, if that's the case, you better let Mike know. I think he's getting jealous." She stopped smiling. "He was looking for you this afternoon."

I looked at her. "Was he mad?"

"He didn't look too happy."

"Ugh," I groaned, leaning my head against the locker.

"What's wrong?"

"We were supposed to try to talk right after school today, but something came up. I gave Jenny a note to pass on to him." I stopped.

"My guess is he didn't get it," Hannah said.

"I don't need this!" I moaned as I pulled my suit on.

"So what were you doing this afternoon?" she asked.

"Registering Sunny for swimming lessons," I said.

"Is he going to make swimming a family tradition and go out for the boys' team?"

"Very funny," I said.

"You never know." Hannah shrugged. "Maybe he'd be good."

We went out on deck, stretched, and then got in for practice. It was a light practice because we had a meet the next day, but I worked it hard, trying to convince myself I had nothing to feel guilty about.

Usually for the short sprint sets, I go third in our lane, because I don't sprint quite as well as they do. Today, however, I went first. I took all my frustration and guilt out on the water, slicing and ripping through it.

I kicked as hard as I could, feeling the water splash down on my back. The black line on the bottom of the pool raced by like my emotions: dark, with a good, straight plan that ended abruptly at a crossing. At the wall, I never bothered to stand up, defog my goggles, or look at anything but our pace clock. I stayed coiled up by the wall, panting and waiting for my interval, ignoring the chatter of my teammates.

When we finished our last set, I was beat. I took my time with my cool-down, mixing in sidestroke, underwaters, and elementary back-stroke. I pushed off and went down in the water, using strong, full pulls, trying to see if I could trace individual water drops as I pushed them from above my head, past my shoulder and hips, down to my toes.

As I pulled myself out of the pool, Coach grinned at me.

"Now that's the kind of workout I like to see!"

"Thanks," I said, resisting the urge to jump back in the pool and hide from my own guilt.

On the way home, I told Sunny he'd start swim lessons on Tuesday. His face lit up. I didn't have the heart to tell him the whole truth, so I decided to wait till Tuesday to tell him someone else would be his instructor.

"Really, Skye?"

"Really."

He grinned the rest of the way home. After dinner, he brought out his Western Civ, and I quizzed him on it. He did really well, and I told him so. He made us cocoa and then took his R. L. Stine book back to his room.

I tried to call both Jenny and Mike, but neither of them were home. It was Mom's turn to work the closing shift at the bar, so I went to bed before she came home. I was kind of relieved, actually. Somehow she always seemed to know when I was trying to hide something.

CHAPTER FOUR

"S kye?"

"Huh?" I looked up from my doodling. Ms. Jenkins was directing the question to me, and with a start I realized the rest of the class was watching me. "I'm sorry, Ms. Jenkins. I didn't hear the question."

She sighed. "Would you please put that away and try to pay attention?"

"Yes, ma'am," I said, putting the paper under my folder. I didn't know what was on it anyway. The day had passed in a blur. I had seen Mike briefly before school and he told me he had gotten my note. He had failed the Shakespeare test, and that was why he had looked upset when Hannah saw him. All I could think about now was today's meet. I was tense, primed, and ready for the 200 free. I kept thinking about the race so much, that in an earlier class I had caught myself breathing on pace.

In a way it was a relief to be so focused on the meet. It made me feel like my old self. I glanced up at the clock, sure that class must be over, only to find that there was still a half hour left.

"I recommend you stay with us in class, Skye," Ms. Jenkins said dryly. "You've got to stay eligible to swim."

"Yes, ma'am," I said again, feeling my cheeks get hot as a few of my classmates snickered.

Fortunately, Ms. Jenkins was in a charitable mood. She redirected the question across the room, and got the answer she was looking for. I really did try to follow the rest of the lecture, but by the time Ms. Jenkins decided we were done and could begin getting ready to leave, I could not have repeated anything from class to save my life.

As I stood up to gather my books together, Steve stepped toward my desk. "Are you all dressed up for the meet?"

I nodded, fidgeting once again with my skirt. I didn't wear skirts often, especially short skirts, and I felt a little uncomfortable. This year our team captains had decided to alternate between dressing up and wearing team shirts on meet days.

Steve nodded back with an appreciative smile. "You look really good."

I smiled. "Thanks." I searched my mind frantically for something nice to say back to him. "Are you getting psyched for basketball season?"

"Yeah," he said. "Will you come to some of our games this year?"

I laughed. "Sure. As long as you come to some of our meets." Swim meets hardly ever drew a crowd. Last year we had tried to make it team policy that each girl brought at least two people to watch each meet, but we gave up halfway through the season. People just didn't care. Volleyball, gymnastics, and football drew the fall season crowds.

Steve shifted in his seat. "What time's your meet?"

"It starts at four."

"Can't make it today," he said, shaking his head.

"How about a week from today?"

"Yeah, I can probably make that, if I know I have a personal invitation."

"You just got one," I said, smiling at him. I knew I was being a terrible flirt, but I didn't really care. I had always thought Steve was cute. And nice. Last year, when we were lab partners in biology, he really treated me like a partner. He thought it was cool that I actually liked the dissecting. And the year before, he and I had done almost all the work for our group presentation in Western Civ. This year, we had three classes together, but since I had started seeing Mike, I hadn't paid that much attention to Steve.

When the bell rang, I bolted out of the row, dodging the other students in the aisle. I was the first one to the door, even though my desk was almost in the back of the classroom. I barely heard Steve as he said, "Good luck, Skye!"

"See you tomorrow," I called back over my shoulder. I was already out the door, so I didn't know if he'd heard me or not.

I didn't wait for Jenny at all, but I knew she'd understand. On meet days I was too wound up to pay attention to anything. I flew through the halls to my locker and stuffed three books into my book bag, hardly even checking to see which ones they were.

I just barely remembered to stop by Hannah's locker. Last year she had been as anxious as I was, but this year she was a lot more mellow. I took a quick look down her row of lockers, knowing I wouldn't wait if she wasn't already there. To my surprise, she was shutting her locker and had her bags in hand.

She looked up at me and grinned. "Ready to kick some Fairview butt?"

"Oh, you better believe it," I said.

We walked quickly outside and over to the pool, clowning around and being obnoxious all the way over there. We had made up a bizarre chant, or maybe it was more of a song that had the refrain of "A splish, a splash, we'll kick some ass!" We were always trying to add more stanzas to it. I barely felt my feet touching the ground as the wind whipped by us, carrying our voices back to the school.

We were laughing and singing when we entered the locker room, and kept it up all the way through the stretches. Coach kept shooting us strange looks and shaking his head, but he didn't tell us to settle down or anything. He knew us too well.

I don't know how it was for the other swimmers, but for me getting hyper before a meet was almost a necessity. If I tried to calm down or be quiet, I'd start thinking too much and make myself sick. This way, bouncing around and being stupid, I kept my mind off my races until I was on the blocks.

"Okay, ladies, we've got lanes one through three for warm-up. Let's get an eight hundred going. Stretch it out, nice and easy, focus on your turns, and don't stop moving!" Coach called.

Warm-ups for meets were always hard because we had to jam the whole team into half the pool to make room for the other team to practice. If one person stopped, everyone had to, because the lanes got so crowded. Hannah and I had claimed lane three, and only the other veterans dared to warm up in our lane with us.

During the first meet of the season, a freshman had gotten in our lane. It wouldn't have been a big deal, if she hadn't stopped suddenly. But not only had she stopped, she'd stopped in the middle of the wall, blocking everyone else's turns. I had just flipped right next to her, barely missing her, and continued my warm-up.

Hannah had yelled at her so loudly, everyone in the pool area knew exactly what had happened. The poor girl had burst into tears as she moved over into another lane. We took our warm-ups seriously on meet days.

"Who wants the honors?" I asked Hannah and Christie as we stood behind the starting block making final adjustments to our caps. Other teammates were making last minute tune-ups behind us.

They both shook their heads. I sighed and stepped up onto the block, snugging my goggles on. I leaned forward at the waist, hands dangling down by my ankles, shaking my arms. I inhaled slowly, and then launched myself off the block.

I hit the water, feeling the tiny air bubbles roll off me as I sliced through the water, and popped up for four quick, powerful strokes. Then I forced myself to slow down and stretch. I focused on my arms, concentrating on each move, making sure my technique was perfect. I slid through the water, not feeling any resistance at all. My legs were taut, pointed toes promising that the upper part of my legs were straight and streamlined behind me, and I barely fluttered my feet up and down.

As I approached the wall, I took my last breath and glided into the wall before I ducked my head and flipped myself over. I twisted coming off the wall, to move to the other side of the lane, and passed Christie and then Hannah. We were all maintaining a distance of just under two feet between each other.

I felt relaxed and good. I could feel the power in my arms and legs, eager to be released, but easily held in check.

We finished our warm-up and moved into our sprint sets, yelling and cheering for each other.

Spectators were beginning to file into the pool area. Sunny was already in his favorite seat. He never missed a meet. Today he was watching us warm up, and I knew his books would stay in his bag. He wouldn't do any homework until we got home tonight.

I had to grin as I remembered my very first high school meet. Sunny had made so much noise cheering for me that the first two times I had gotten on the block, the referee had had to ask us all to stand down while he went over to Sunny to tell him to be quiet. The second time, the ref had threatened to kick Sunny out if he didn't calm down. I thought I would die of embarrassment.

Now Sunny knows that as soon as the swimmers step up onto the blocks, he has to be quiet until the gun goes off. He yells for everyone on our team, but whenever I'm behind the blocks, his cheers are almost deafening. When I'm in the water, I can't hear anyone yelling except for him. Although it's still a little embarrassing, actually, I love it. I'm used to it now. It's nice to know that someone cares.

Mom tries to get time off for my meets, but it rarely seems to work out. I've gotten good at pretending that it doesn't matter she's missed nearly every one of my meets. I know she feels bad enough already. She doesn't need me complaining about it.

After warm-up we climbed out of the water and grabbed our towels as we headed to the locker room for our team meeting. Once again, I scanned the bleachers as I walked by. Sunny grinned hugely at me and waved. I waved back, but I couldn't quite grin. Mike still wasn't here. I pulled my sweatshirt over my head and wrapped a towel around my waist.

We shivered in the locker room as Coach went over the lineup one last time. There were always a couple of last minute changes. I would be in the 200 and 400 yard freestyle relays, as well as in the 200 and 500 yard freestyle events. I was glad Coach hadn't put me in the 200 medley relay. This way, my first event was the 200 free, and that was the one I had the best chance of getting a state qualifying time for.

Back out on the warm deck, we did our team cheer, and then stood quietly and listened to three girls sing the national anthem a cappella. Then the meet began.

The 200 free is always the second event of the meet, so I went to the farthest corner of our team area and sat down. With my towel wrapped around me like a blanket, I put my back against the wall and drew my knees up in front of me. I bent my head down and closed my eyes, breathing deeply, visualizing my race. I felt the cold water of the start, the fast flip and push of my turns, the burning in my lungs on the last lap, and I saw my time when I finished.

I wanted to make state qualification more than anything. I had been training and working for it since the beginning of my freshman year. I had thought I might make it that year. Last year I had been *sure* I would make it. Everyone said I'd make it this year, but I hadn't yet. *What if I never do?* I thought. *What if I spend all four years in high school trying to make state, and simply can't do it?* Swimming was the scholarship ticket I wanted. My grade point was good—3.76—but it wasn't enough for a full scholarship.

Dimly I heard my teammates start calling LaTonya's name. She swam the butterfly leg of our medley relay team, so I knew the race was almost over. I pulled my cap on, and grabbed my goggles. I went up to Coach to get my entry card.

He held on to it before giving it to me. "What's your best time?"

"2:06.61."

"What's state qual?"

"2:05 flat."

"How are you going to drop time?"

"Work my turns, pay attention to my pace, and not hold anything back in the last fifty."

He nodded. "Their girl in lane four goes about a 2:06 also, so you two should push each other. Stay with her pace," he added as he finally gave me the card.

I went back behind the blocks and congratulated the members of our relay team on their win, trying to ignore the butterflies in my stomach. It didn't seem to matter that I swam this race at almost every meet. I still felt sick to my stomach right before it each time.

Hannah had swum the breaststroke leg of the relay. She stopped beside me, dripping and panting. "Good luck," she said between breaths.

"Thanks. You did a great job," I said.

She shrugged, but she also grinned, looking past me to the stands. In the middle of her grin, she kind of froze. "Oh, no!"

"What? What's wrong?"

"Lou's here. I can't believe he showed up!"

Even though I really didn't want to think about Hannah's love life right before my event, I had to laugh. Lou hadn't missed a meet since they had started dating. "Are you going to say hello to him?"

"No way!" she exclaimed. "I didn't invite him. I told him I didn't want to see him anymore." She shook her head. "He keeps calling my house. He won't leave me alone."

"And you love it," I told her flatly.

She glared at me and then followed the rest of the relay team over to Coach Sullivan.

I gave my card to the timer and stood behind block three, swinging my arms in big circles. Then I bent at the waist and touched my palms to the ground, keeping my knees straight. My stomach felt like it was ready to lift off for Mars. I knew that it was just nerves; if I ran to the bathroom to throw up, nothing would happen. In spite of all my experience, I was still as nervous as a freshman. I paced back and forth anxiously.

The referee blew his whistle, and I stepped up onto the block, pulling my goggles over my eyes. I focused inside. I was aware of what was going on around me only because it had happened so often before.

"Ladies, this is the 200 yard freestyle," the announcer reminded us, "Eight lengths of the pool. Mr. Starter."

I had my head bent down and was still shaking my arms out, but I could picture the starter in my mind's eye as he lifted the gun up over his head.

"Take your mark."

I bent at the waist and just a little at the knees, grabbing the underside of the block. My nose was almost touching my knees. The gun went off and so did we.

I threw everything I could into my start, lifting my head to get as much height and distance as I could, stretching my arms forward as if I could reach the far side of the pool from my start.

Just before I hit the water I tucked my chin, slicing down just a couple of feet, and kicked as hard as I could all the way to the surface. I pulled six times before I dared to take a breath. Turning my head to the left, I could see the girl in lane four, the one I had to beat, matching my strokes. On the next breath, I turned to the right. The girl in lane two was right with us. We pulled into the first turn together, and I gained just a little on her off the wall. She caught back up in two strokes. Lane four was still with us. The rest of the pack had dropped off.

Our opening pace was good and fast. I was pushing it, but I knew I had plenty left to give in the rest of the race. Breathe, pull, pull, breathe, pull, and I flipped over again.

Into the second turn, we were all still together. I came off the wall and gained a foot lead. This time they let me keep it. I usually swam the 200 freestyle with a fast opening fifty, but then I'd ease it back on the second fifty just a little before bringing home the last hundred as hard as I could. Not today. Today I had almost two seconds to drop.

I was still in the lead coming off the third turn, but then the girl in lane four moved back up with me as we hit the fourth turn. Lane two was hanging back.

I could barely wait for the gulp of air as we finished the fifth turn. I tried to breathe too early and inhaled a little water. I forced my coughing to stay underwater, but started breathing every other stroke, trying to get my wind back. Breathe, pull, breathe, pull, breathe, pull, pull, breathe. I was finally back in rhythm.

When we hit the sixth turn, the girl in lane four had a foot lead on me. Lane two was clearly out of the running. My legs were screaming in pain, my lungs burned, and I couldn't even feel my arms as they smacked the water. I tucked my chin down and tried to shift into overdrive.

Suddenly, I saw feet in front of us, a couple of lanes over. I almost panicked before I realized that we were lapping the rest of the pool.

Inch by painful little inch, I moved up till I was even with lane four. We were going into the last turn. I knew I could get the lead back on this turn, but I also knew that I would have to ignore my body's demand for air in order to keep it.

As I approached the end of the lane, I took that last breath, ducked my head down, and threw my body over into the turn. I didn't wait for my feet to hit the wall before I started to kick out. I held my arms above my head in such a tight streamline it hurt. I kicked my feet, envisioning them working as fast as pistons.

I took four strokes off the wall before I dared to breathe on my left side, looking for lane four. She was just behind me. I put everything I had into each stroke, grabbing the water and shoving it behind me, kicking hard and feeling the splash come back down on my back. I saw the black line end in a large T, and shoved my arm forward to the wall. As I lifted my head up, I saw lane four touch the wall. I had done part of what I set out to do. I had won the race.

"Good job," I said, leaning over to the swimmer in lane four.

"Thanks," she said with a tired smile. We shook hands and then I turned to congratulate lane two.

I could hear Sunny, still hollering. I turned and faced the bleachers and waved to him before I put a finger over my lips. He quieted down. A little.

I knew my time was good, but I was still afraid to ask. I had worked so hard. I wasn't sure my time really felt fast enough.

"What was my time?" I panted, looking up to the timer.

"2:05.43." The timer said.

"Oh no!" I threw my head back and just floated on top of the water for a minute. I let the silent tears slip out of the corners of my eyes and mix with the pool water. So close. It was bittersweet. I had won, and I had dropped time, but once again state qual had eluded me. It seemed that my time would never come.

I stayed out in the pool as long as I could, trying to cool down. My face was on fire. Most people don't think about swimmers getting hot and sweaty, but we do. I took my cap off and felt the cold water sink in through my hair to my scalp. I ducked underwater again, rinsing the tears off my face. Coach got really angry with us if we were poor sports about our times. I had, after all, won and improved my time. I tried to feel good about that, but it wasn't enough.

Pulling myself out of the pool took considerable effort. I felt like every little cell in my body was drained. Christie was standing behind lane three, waiting for her 200 individual medley.

"Almost, Skye," she said, giving me a hug. "You'll get it next time."

"Thanks," I said, hugging her back. "I sure hope so."

I turned to walk back over to Coach, and heard a low whistle directly behind me. "Now there's a nice butt!"

I spun around. "Mike!" I reached up for a hug.

"Hey! Congratulations on the win!" he said, smiling. He started to hug me, but then tried to draw back at the last minute. "Can we wait till you dry off?" he asked.

"Nope," I said, pulling him in for a quick hug. I laughed when I stepped away and saw how wet I had gotten his T-shirt. I wanted to feel his strong arms around me again.

"You have any soap? I might as well take my shower right here," he said with a laugh.

"You can't take a shower out here," I said, teasing. "I don't want everybody else seeing your body."

"So you want to take a private shower with me sometime?" he asked, dropping his voice so no one else could hear. His eyes were an intense blue. I could see the desire in them, and I wondered if I looked as awkward as I suddenly felt. I had been joking, but I realized he was serious.

I laughed nervously and stepped away from him. "Come on, I want to get my towel. I'm cold."

"I noticed," he murmured.

I tried not to think about that as he followed me over to the team area. I also tried not to think about him watching me walk in front of him. It was hard to ignore, considering the way he kept going "Mmm, mmm, mmmm!"

I grabbed my towel and wrapped it around my waist as quickly as I could, and then I pulled my sweatshirt over my head in a flurry. Mike still managed to put his arm around me so fast that his hand was on my side underneath the sweatshirt.

"How about another hug?" he asked, pulling me into him.

"Mmmm," I sighed into his ear. "I've missed you lately."

"You have? Maybe we should go out tonight after the meet."

I didn't answer him right away. I knew I couldn't go, but I didn't want to destroy the mood. "How much of the race did you get to see?"

"Just the last part," he said. "Enough to see you win. Pretty cool."

I laughed again. "It was okay. The wins and places don't matter as much as the times do, though."

"How was your time?" he asked.

"It was my best time so far," I said with a big grin.

"Good! Did you make it to regionals?"

"State," I said gently. "Swimmers go to state; track and tennis go to regionals."

"Oh. Did you make it to state?"

"Not quite, but I'm closer than I was."

He shrugged. "I'm sure you'll make it next time," he said, dismissing the subject.

"Hey, Skye," Hannah said, coming up from behind us. "Awesome job, girl!" She grabbed me away from Mike and spun me into a hug. "State's just around the corner for you!" She lowered her voice. "Coach wants to see you."

I nodded. "I'll be right back, Mike. Hannah, will you keep him company?"

"As if you had to ask," Hannah said with a mischievous smile.

"Now be good, both of you," I said, wagging my finger at them. We all laughed. I walked over to see Coach. I knew I had to anyway. He always wanted us to check in with him both before and after each race.

"Hey, Coach," I said. "Didn't quite make it."

He grinned at me and shook his head. "No, but you're closer than you were. You did a real nice job!"

I grinned in spite of myself. "Thanks."

He consulted his clipboard. "You dropped off your pace just a little bit on that third fifty," he said.

"I'm sure I did," I said. "I tried to swallow the pool coming off the turn."

He laughed. "I keep telling you girls not to do that. When will you ever listen?"

"I'm sorry. It's just that I was so thirsty!"

He laughed again, but then he got kind of serious. "Um, Skye, I really don't want to have to get on your case, but—"

"I know, I know," I broke in quickly. "Mike's going to go sit on the bleachers. We just came over here to grab my towel."

Coach nodded. "I'm glad to hear that he'll be with the spectators where he belongs. Just remember that you're supposed to be with the team, where you belong."

"Sure thing," I said, feeling a little uncomfortable.

I went back over to Mike and Hannah. "I heard you and Lou broke up," Mike was saying.

"Yeah," she said in a bored tone. "We did."

"I thought I saw his car in the parking lot."

I laughed from behind him and slipped my arm around his waist. "You did. Hannah's so irresistible that he can't stay away."

"I know how Lou feels," Mike said, looking at me.

"You find Hannah irresistible?" I asked innocently.

Hannah groaned. "I'm leaving now. I don't need to cause problems between you two."

I took Mike by the hand and led him over to the bleachers. I headed toward some empty seats a few rows behind Sunny.

"Skye! You were great!" he hollered, jumping up and down as we passed by.

"Thanks, Sunny," I said. "I'm right here, you know. You don't have to yell." I knew it wouldn't do any good though. During meets, he yelled everything.

"You're the fastest swimmer!" he shouted.

I just kind of grinned and nodded at him. He always told me I was great and then said I was the fastest swimmer he ever saw, even if someone had just beaten me.

"What's next?" he asked me, ignoring Mike.

"The next one I'm in is the 200 free relay."

"Okay," he said, and then he turned back around and started cheering for our team again.

Mike and I went up a couple of rows and sat down.

"How much longer till the relay?" Mike asked.

"Well, we've got one more swimming event, then we have diving, then three more events. I've probably got between a half hour and forty-five minutes before I swim again."

He put his arm around my waist, sliding his hand in under my sweatshirt again. He pulled me close, wrapping his arm around me till his palm was over my belly button. He let his fingers slide down a little. Suddenly I was having a hard time breathing. "Let's go take a walk somewhere," he whispered in my ear.

He made me want to forget everything I was supposed to do and do things I had only heard about. But I was afraid. I was afraid of being caught, or of something going wrong.

I shook my head and tried to inch away from him a little without making a big deal about it. My heart was racing as if I had just finished a sprint set. "I've got to go back over to the team. Coach wants us staying together during meets."

"Then why'd you bring me over here?" he asked. He had relaxed his arm, and now it was just loose around me and his hand was on my hip.

"Because he won't let spectators stay in the team area."

"Let me get this straight. I can't be over there and you can't be over here?"

"Basically, yes."

He shook his head. "Then why am I even here?"

I just looked at him for a minute, hurt. "To cheer for me and to support me."

"I bet you can't even hear me when you're in the water."

"Not very well," I admitted. "But I'll know you're here."

He sighed and rolled his eyes. "How much longer will the meet last?"

"It'll be over around six."

He stared at me. "Are we going out after?"

I looked away. "You know I can't."

"Well, I guess I left practice early for nothing then."

"I thought you came to watch me swim because it's important to me. When I watch you play football, I never get to sit with you on the bench."

"That's different! I'm out on the field. Besides, football's fun to watch. This is just—"

"Just what?" I demanded.

"Nothing," he muttered. He seemed to realize for the first time that I was angry. "C'mon, Skye. You know I came here to be with you."

I didn't say anything. I was too mad to speak.

We sat there in a very uncomfortable silence for a few minutes.

"Can you at least walk me out to my car?" he finally asked.

"No," I snapped. I stood up and stomped down the bleachers.

I didn't look back till I was on the other side of the pool with the rest of my team. When I did glance back, he was already gone. *Maybe I should have gone to the car with him,* I thought. *A few minutes wouldn't have hurt anything. What am I so afraid of? All the other girls would jump at a chance to be with him.*

I sat down among the towels and sweatpants scattered on the deck.

Hannah was the only one brave enough to come over to me. "Are you okay?"

I couldn't talk. All I could do was shake my head.

"You want to talk about it?"

I shook my head again.

Hannah looked at me carefully for a minute. "Should I stay here or do you want to be left alone?"

Swallowing hard, I looked around. "Come sit with me for diving."

We sat to the side, away from the rest of the team, during the diving competition. Hannah started making fun of Lou, who was sitting all by himself in the bleachers, but she finally realized it didn't make me feel any better to hear about her guy who couldn't stay away from her even when he was told to. When I told her I thought she really wanted to go sit with him, she got mad, so I knew I was right. To change the subject, she started in on her ridiculous sportscaster analysis of the dives. At least it helped me get my mind off Mike.

"And now for Fairview, we have the slender carrot-topped girl whose name I can't pronounce," she said in a dramatic undertone. "She's stepping toward the ladder. Will she make it onto the board? Yes, she does! Now, can she really do a twist in the air? Let's watch and find out."

We watched as the diver stared fiercely at the end of the board, clenching and unclenching her fists.

"Oh, this must be a difficult dive, folks," Hannah intoned. "Here she goes, she's taking that first step...nice measured pace...good bounce. But, oh, I don't think she's got enough for the rotation." Everyone in the pool area moaned in sympathetic pain as the diver belly flopped loudly.

In spite of Hannah's attempts to cheer me up, the rest of the meet was awful for me. I had the slowest split I had ever had for the 200 free relay. In the 500 free I took fourth, and my time was the slowest I had gone in the last year.

Coach decided that I must have given too much for the 200 free, so he pulled me out of the 400 free relay to give the team a better chance. I didn't bother to tell him that I was upset about my boyfriend. He just didn't understand that kind of thing.

I didn't really understand, either.

CHAPTER FIVE

In the locker room, I dawdled. I took a long time in the showers and got dressed slowly. Christie wanted to know what I thought was going to happen between Hannah and Lou. Hannah hadn't stayed to shower after the meet, and had been seen leaving with him. Christie was disappointed with my lack of interest in Hannah's love life. It was the talk of the team. I tried to tell her that because of my last races, I wasn't feeling very good. And that's what I tried to tell myself, too.

I was the last one out of the locker room. I didn't want to see anyone or talk to anyone. I just wanted to be alone, so I could examine my misery.

Sunny was waiting for me, but I ignored his cheery "Hi, Skye!" when I came out into the lobby. I saw that Tony was the guard working the desk.

"Hey," I said hesitantly to him, "I know this sounds a little weird, but did anyone leave a message for me or call or anything?"

"No," Tony said, shaking his head.

"How long have you been out here?"

He shrugged. "Since the beginning of the meet."

"Oh. Okay. Thanks."

I turned and started toward the door. "Come on, Sunny, let's go."

"Hang on, Skye, I want to show you something."

I groaned. "Sunny, come on! I really just want to get home, okay? I'm hungry, and I'm tired...." I leaned my forehead against the cold hard door and muttered to myself, "I'm a mess. Everything's a mess."

"Please, Skye," Sunny begged. "Please come here."

I dropped my bag to the floor in front of the door and walked back over to where Sunny was waiting by the candy machine.

"I don't have any money, if that's what you're after," I said.

He shook his head. "I can't decide what to get," he said, grinning at me as if he had just told me he had won a million dollars. "Should I get M&M's or the Sugar Babies?"

"They're both good, Sunny." They were also both my favorites, but my stomach was twisted, and I didn't even want to look at the machine. "Just pick one and let's get going, okay?"

"But which one?" he persisted. When Sunny had an idea or problem, he was like a bulldog. You just couldn't make him let go of it.

"I don't care, Sunny. It's your candy."

"But I can't decide!"

"If you don't just pick one, I'll pick it for you, and then I'll eat half of it," I warned.

"Okay." He nodded agreeably. "Which one?"

I sighed again. "Put the money in," I said.

He trustingly reached up and dropped the quarters in. "Okay, pick one."

"Okay," I said. I reached out like I was going to hit the Sugar Babies button, but at the last second I swerved and hit the SweeTarts button instead.

His face fell and his heavy brows drew together. "Why'd you do that?"

I shrugged, turning back toward the door. "Because I wanted to," I said. "Now come on. I want to get home."

I heard him pulling the SweeTarts out of the machine. He caught up with me at the door and tried to hand me the candy.

"No, thanks," I said, shaking my head. "You bought them."

"I know," he said, grinning from ear to ear. "I bought them for you."

"What?" I stopped and looked at him. Money and candy were both huge special treats for Sunny. He never shared.

He laughed and did a little dance step. "I bought them for you," he said. "'Cause you did so good today." He was still holding out the candy toward me. "It's for you," he repeated.

I reached out slowly and took the roll from him. Amazingly, his smile got even bigger.

"I surprised you, huh?" He was positively delighted with himself. "I thought Sugar Babies and M&M's were your favorites. I'm glad I didn't just get one of them. I didn't even think about the SweeTarts. This way you got just what you wanted."

I felt like an absolute jerk. The only reason I had picked the SweeTarts was because I thought he wouldn't want them. I had been trying to hurt him while he had been trying to do something special for me. My stomach tightened up even more.

I reached out and pulled him into a hug, desperately fighting back the tears. He hugged me back fiercely. "You're the best swimmer," he said for about the hundredth time, but it was the first time I realized that he truly believed that.

Breaking the roll of SweeTarts in half, I said, "Eating candy by yourself isn't any fun." I usually used that line when I was trying to get candy away from him, but this time I really meant it. I held out the half roll, and with a bashful grin, he took it from me.

"You did really great today," he said again, as he popped the candy into his mouth. He made a face at the sour taste.

"Not really," I said with a sigh.

"You won!" he said, looking at me in disbelief. "You can't do any better than that."

I shook my head. "I won one race, but I lost the other two. Coach didn't even let me swim all my events. Besides," I groaned, "I still didn't make state."

"You will," he said, skipping just a little.

"Oh, yeah?"

He nodded. "Yep."

"How do you know?" I asked, trying to hide my smile. Sometimes he really was like a little six year old.

"'Cause you're the best," he said simply, "and that's all that matters."

We were taking our usual route home, which passed by our old elementary school. The sun was setting right behind it. I stopped to watch the red clouds for a moment. Sunny went on another three steps before he realized I wasn't with him anymore.

"Skye?" he asked as he turned around and looked back at me.

"Want to go swinging?" I asked suddenly. I wanted to feel like a kid again.

He gave me a huge grin and took two quick steps forward. Then he stopped suddenly and his grin disappeared, just as if someone had hit the delete key on a computer. It was replaced by a frown.

"We're supposed to go straight home," he said uncertainly. "Mom'll worry if we're not home when she calls."

"We won't stay long." I smiled at him and tried unsuccessfully to raise just one eyebrow. "Besides, we can always tell Mom that the meet went a little late."

He still didn't look sure.

"I won't tell if you won't tell," I said softly.

He started grinning again, and his head started nodding up and down like it was on a spring.

"Race you," I said.

He took a deep breath and then took off as fast as he could toward the playground. I broke into a light jog and stayed just a few feet behind him. The trees had lost most of their leaves and we crunched loudly under the graying sky. His lumbering gait was almost painful for me to watch, because I knew he was trying so hard.

Every once in a while I'd say, "I'm catching up, Sunny," or "Better watch it, I'm gonna get you!" Each time I said something, he'd put on a little burst of speed, but I could easily keep up with him.

We hit the gravel of the playground, and we both stopped. Sunny turned to me, panting and grinning in the twilight.

"I won!"

"You sure did," I said. "I guess that means I have to push first."

"Yep!" he cried. He dropped his bag and ran over to the swings.

I pushed him for about ten minutes. He loved it. Swinging was one of his favorite activities. We used to go to the playground every weekend, but I hadn't had much time in the last year or so.

After a while, I sat down in the swing next to him. He started to slow down. "I'll come push you in a minute, Skye," he said.

I shook my head. "That's okay, Sunny. Let's just swing by ourselves, okay?"

He looked at me. "Really?"

"Really."

We kept swinging in silence for a few minutes. I zoned out, listening to the chains squeak every time Sunny went forward, and the gnashing of the gravel when he let his feet drag over it. I wasn't really swinging, more like just drifting, enjoying the cool fall air.

I tried to think about what I'd say to Mike the next time I saw him, but then I decided I didn't want to think about him at all. As soon as I decided that, however, I couldn't get him out of my mind. He could be so nice and sincere one minute, and an absolute jerk the next. The longer we went out, though, the more of the jerk I was seeing, and the less of the nice guy.

True, he had left practice early to come to the meet, but then he didn't stay. Even though I don't particularly like football, I had been to both home football games this year, just to watch him play.

My thoughts wandered to his strong arms, and dark blue eyes, soft lips, and broad chest.... I sighed. I had had a crush on him for so long, dating him was supposed to be a dream come true. What was wrong? Was it him, or was it me?

"Skye?" Sunny said softly.

I looked around and realized that he had stopped swinging. It was full dark. "Oh, wow," I said, "we'd better get going!"

He nodded and we headed for our bags. I didn't have to encourage him to walk fast the rest of the way home. He kept up without complaining. When we got home, the clock said 6:45. I checked the answering machine and sighed with relief when I saw there weren't any messages on it. Mom hadn't called yet.

As if on cue, the phone rang.

"Hello?"

"Hi, honey, how'd your meet go?"

"Pretty good," I said, quietly opening the cabinets, looking for dinner food.

"How good is pretty good?"

"Um...." I was scanning the cabinet. "I dropped time in my 200."

"How much?"

"Not enough," I said.

"Skye, don't get all negative now," Mom warned. "If you dropped time, then you're closer than you were. Besides, you're the one who always says every second counts, remember?"

"I know, I know." I found a can of ravioli and then pulled out a pan.

"What did you and Sunny have for dinner?"

"Ravioli," I said, easing open the refrigerator door.

"Is that all?"

"And salad," I said, grabbing the lettuce.

"Sunny's favorite." I could tell she was smiling. "Okay," Mom said. "Well, I've got to close at the bar tonight, so don't wait up."

"Okay," I said. "Don't work too hard, and don't take any grief."

She laughed. "Thanks, honey. Sleep well."

"Good night, Mom."

We hung up.

Sunny came wandering back into the kitchen. "What's for dinner?"

"Ravioli and salad."

"Cool," he said.

"Why don't you get the drinks?" I suggested.

"Okay." He went to the fridge and found a Diet Coke for me and pulled out the milk for himself. He poured the milk in a glass and returned the carton. Then he got some napkins out and carried everything into the living room.

"We missed *Friends*," he called.

"Find something else good," I called back. "It'll be ready in a minute."

He found another sitcom on TV. We ate dinner, and then he surprised me for the second time that evening. I started to get up with my plate, when he said, "Sit down. I'll do them." He picked up my plate along with his own, and took them into the kitchen.

I listened to him rattle around in the kitchen. He usually avoided doing dishes whenever he could. Only when I had a lot of energy would I try to get him to do them. Since I cooked, he was supposed to do the dishes, but he fought me every step of the way. I gave up asking him a long time ago. Whenever I did ask him and he said no, he'd always have an excuse ready for Mom if I told. Either he was really tired that night or he had too much homework. Mom only got angry when I said she always took his side. Eventually I quit fighting. It was easier just to do the dishes myself.

While Sunny was finishing the dishes, the phone rang.

"Got it," I called. "Hello?" I said into the phone.

"Are you still talking to me?" Mike said into my ear.

"I don't think so," I replied, feeling my stomach clench up inside. I couldn't believe the effect his voice had on me.

"Why not?" he asked, almost whispering.

"You know why." I was determined not to give in.

"Come on, Skye. Give me a chance." His voice switched back to its normal tone.

"Why should I?"

"Because...."

"Because why?"

"Because we're great together and you know it."

"That's lame," I began, in spite of my flip-flopping stomach. How did he always know when to say just what I wanted to hear?

"Look, Skye, I'm sorry about this afternoon, okay? I thought we'd go out after the meet like we did after the game last week. When I found out I wasn't going to be able to spend time with you, I was really upset. I'm sorry."

It took all my willpower not to say anything.

"Skye? Please? Come on, I'm begging here."

"Can I get that in writing?" I asked, stalling. I didn't want to forgive him; I knew in my mind that I shouldn't, but my heart was in a puddle just from hearing his voice.

"My word should be good enough," he said stiffly.

I sighed. "Mike, you *know* I can't go out on school nights. I'm tired of fighting about it."

"I don't know. It seems like you could get out some nights, if you tried. If you really wanted to," he said sulkily.

"Believe me, the first chance I get, you'll know. But for now, I'm tired of fighting."

"I'm sorry," he repeated. It didn't sound very genuine to me, but I was afraid to push the issue. I didn't want to make him mad. He was my first boyfriend. He could get any girl in the school.

We were both quiet for a second.

"So, am I forgiven or what?" he asked finally.

"Yeah, I guess. This time," I added.

"That's all I need. There won't be a next time."

"Good," I said. I was so happy I did a little dance right there in the kitchen.

"So how'd the rest of the meet go?"

"We won," I said.

"How'd your other races go?"

"Not too great," I admitted.

"Then I guess it's a good thing I didn't stay," he said with a laugh.

I bit my tongue. I wasn't going to let him know that he could upset me enough to affect my swimming.

"Well, I hate to say this, but I've got to get going. I've got a physics test," I said. "See you tomorrow?"

"Yeah, sure. I'll see you tomorrow."

"Okay. Bye."

"Bye."

I hung up the phone and just stared at it. Sometimes I made myself really mad. I didn't even know what I wanted. A few minutes ago I had been missing him, and then I had been psyched that he had called. I had been happy when he apologized, but now that the phone call was over, I just felt really annoyed. I paced back and forth behind the couch.

Sunny came back into the living room. "Who was that?"

"Nobody," I said.

"Mike?"

"Does it matter?" I snapped.

"It *was* Mike," he said to himself, shaking his head.

"What's your problem?"

He shrugged and didn't say anything. Instead he picked up the TV guide and started looking through it.

"Is your homework done?" I demanded.

"Most of it."

"Why don't you go finish it, and then watch TV?"

He frowned at me. "I'd rather watch TV now."

I was too tired to argue. "Okay. For a half hour. Then you have to go do your work."

"Okay," he said.

"Pick a good show," I said. I went to the kitchen and checked the freezer. We both loved Fudgsicles, but there was only one left. There was barely enough vanilla ice cream for two small bowls. I checked the fridge, but we were out of chocolate syrup.

I sighed and scooped the last of the ice cream into bowls anyway. Then, as I was about to carry them out to the living room, inspiration struck. I sprinkled hot chocolate mix on top of the ice cream.

Sunny smiled halfheartedly at me when I handed him the bowl, but frowned when he picked up the spoon. "What's this stuff on top?"

"Hot chocolate."

"What?"

"Just try it, okay?"

He grumbled a little, but he ate it. When we finished, I went to pick up his bowl. "Admit it, it wasn't that bad."

He shrugged.

I rolled my eyes and went to the kitchen. I put the bowls in the dishwasher, and quickly rearranged some of the dishes Sunny had put in so they'd wash better. Then I started the dishwasher.

When I got back out to the living room, Sunny was still slumped in his corner of the couch. We were both silent till the next commercial.

"What's your problem all of a sudden?" I demanded.

He shrugged and sank even lower into the couch.

"Come on, Sunny, give."

He shook his head and his lower lip started to stick out, a sure sign that he was pouting.

"Sunny, come on. Why are you all upset now? You were happy before."

He kept his eyes on the TV.

I waited for a minute. "Why are you so bothered that Mike called?"

He just shrugged again, but he also kind of scrunched up his eyes, and I knew I was right.

"Why don't you like Mike?" I persisted.

"Shhh, the show's starting again."

I turned the volume down and then stood right in front of the TV.

"Why don't you like Mike?"

"Skye! Come on!" He leaned over on the couch, trying to see around me to the TV. "You promithed! I get to watch TV for a half hour!"

I shifted every time he moved so I was always blocking his view. "Tell me why you don't like Mike."

"I never thaid I don't like him."

"Then what's wrong?"

He crossed his arms and put his chin on his chest. His pudgy face was all mushed together in a frown.

"Come on, Sunny, all you have to do is tell me what's wrong."

He stood up, and I shifted again, prepared to block him. He went around the couch and headed down the hall to his room. When he got to his door, he turned around and looked at me. I could see the tears running down his cheeks.

"Mike ith mean!" he said. "And now that you're going out with him, you're being mean too!" he shouted. He stepped into his room, then slammed the door.

I sat down on the couch and stared at the TV without turning the volume back up.

Why would Sunny say that? It's not like he had ever had a class with Mike, or had hung out in the cafeteria with him. I decided that Jenny was right. Sunny was just jealous that I wanted to spend time with Mike.

When I finished studying, I called Jenny, but no one was home. She and her parents had probably gone out to dinner after her gymnastics meet.

I stayed in front of the quiet TV, trying to figure out what I was going to do. I still didn't have any answers when I finally went to bed.

CHAPTER
SIX

I was waiting for Sunny to pack up his books for school when the doorbell rang. I couldn't believe it when I opened the door and saw Mike standing there with two red carnations.

"Hi," he said, handing me the flowers. "I was hoping you'd let me give you a ride to school."

"Thanks," I said, a little flustered. "That'd be great. I'll get my stuff."

"Hey, Skye," Mike said before I could turn around. "You know...I just wanted to tell you...I like you so much...it makes me...it makes me crazy when I can't be with you. You're so different from the other girls I've dated. It's not easy taking things slowly with someone like you."

I felt my face flush when he leaned over and brushed his lips against my cheek. Just then I heard Sunny clomping down the hall. I whirled around and grabbed my books.

"We've got a ride to school, Sunny," I said in a cheery voice. "We won't have to walk this morning."

Sunny just frowned and pushed his way out the door.

As we walked out to the car, Mike tried to joke, saying, "Hey, Sunny, cheer up! I don't bite, and I'm saving your legs a trip."

Sunny refused to be cheered. "I'd rather walk," he sulked.

"Fine," Mike said, opening the passenger door for me. "Walk to school."

Sunny turned away from us. "Okay." He started walking down the sidewalk.

"Sunny!" I called.

"Just let him go," Mike said.

I shook my head. "I can't. Mom would positively kill me if anything happened to him."

"Nothing's going to happen," he said.

"Sunny!" I yelled again.

He stopped.

"Come on," I called. "It's just a ride to school. We'll be late if we walk."

Even though he was thirty yards away, I could see his shoulders slowly rise and then fall in his classic huge sigh. He trudged back to us. We climbed into the car and rode silently to school.

~

Mom got off early Saturday night, so I was able to go out. Mike and I went to the movies and he was a complete gentleman. We held hands during the show, and we parked at the end of the block for a little while before he dropped me off in time for my curfew. The date was so perfect I floated through our family trip to the bowling alley on Sunday afternoon.

Monday, I overslept, which is never a good way to start the week. We had to rush to get ready, and Sunny isn't very happy if his routine is disturbed in any way. He was grumbling even before I opened the front door to discover Mike waiting for us by the curb.

"Hey!" I said, grinning foolishly. "You didn't tell me you were picking us up again today."

"That would have ruined the surprise," Mike said, kissing me on the cheek.

I loved pulling into the school parking lot, me with my hand on Mike's knee, him with his arm around my shoulders. I knew that a lot of other girls were wishing they were me.

As soon as we stopped, Sunny undid his seat belt and bolted out of the car. He practically ran into the school.

"Hey," I said to Mike as we slowly walked hand and hand into the school. "You know, I love it when you pick us up, but you don't have to tomorrow."

"And why not?" he asked. "Is your other boyfriend showing up in a cooler car?"

I laughed. "I don't have another boyfriend, and you know it. But tomorrow I get my mom's car."

He whistled. "How'd you pull that off?"

I gave him a playful little shove. "It was part of my deal with Mom."

"What deal?" he asked, holding the school door open for me.

I looked up at him and smiled. "Well, if you'll let me take you to McDonald's tomorrow night around five, I'll explain the deal then."

His eyebrows practically disappeared under his bangs, they arched so high. "Are you asking me to go out with you on a school night?"

I nodded, grinning from ear to ear.

He clutched at his chest dramatically. "I think," he gasped, "I'm having a heart attack."

I shook my head and turned to go to my locker. "If you die, I guess you can't go with me."

He grabbed my arm and swung me back around to him before I could take a step, pulling me close and tight. "Nothing would make me miss a chance to be with you," he said directly into my ear. Then he started kissing my neck.

"Mike!" I hissed.

"What?" he murmured. His lips started moving across my jaw.

"People are—" He stopped me with a full kiss. His mouth was open. His tongue was soft, and for a moment I felt like I was melting in his arms. I gradually became aware of the other people milling around in the hall, opening and shutting their lockers. I tried to pull away, remembering all those times I had criticized other couples for making out in the halls. He wouldn't let me go.

"Mike! Stop it, please," I begged and pushed at him.

He stopped instantly, and basically dropped me. He turned on his heel and walked down the hall away from me, without saying anything.

Jenny came up from behind me. "Thanks a lot, Skye," she said.

"Huh?"

"I thought we were best friends." She followed my gaze after Mike, disappearing in the crowd.

I turned and stared at her. "We are best friends. What do you mean?"

She shrugged. "It's no big deal, Skye. I mean, everybody in school seems to know about it but me."

"Seems to know what?"

Jenny had started walking toward our lockers, and I hurried after her. "Jenny? What are you talking about?"

She opened her locker without saying anything. She wouldn't even look at me.

"Jenny!" I demanded. "Would you please tell me what's going on?" I was completely bewildered.

Shaking her head, Jenny said, "Best friends tell each other things."

I dropped my backpack onto the floor and took a deep breath. "Jenny, I do tell you everything. I have absolutely no idea what's going on here."

She finally looked at me. "Like you've told me about you and Mike?" she asked.

"Yes!" I said, nodding. "Like I've told you about me and Mike."

"What about you and Mike?"

"About how much I like him. About how he asked me out. About our first kiss. Jenny," I said, shaking my head now, "I feel like I'm defending myself, and I haven't done anything."

She gave me a funny look. "So you tell me all about that stuff, but you don't tell me when you finally sleep with him?"

I blinked. "If I sleep with him, I'm pretty sure you'll be one of the first people to hear about it."

Her face flooded with relief, but then she frowned. "What do you mean, 'if'?"

"I mean, *if*. What else would I mean?"

Jenny closed her locker and looked at me. "You haven't slept with him?"

I shook my head.

She took a deep breath. "Skye, people have been telling me that you and Mike have been sleeping together."

"They what?"

She made a face. "People have been saying you two are doing it."

I leaned my head back against the lockers. "Where do people get this?" I lifted my head and looked at Jenny. "I know some people just make assumptions, and that's bad enough, but I had no idea people were actually saying that!"

"I'm sorry, Skye," Jenny said miserably. "I should have trusted you."

"How could you believe that?" I shook my head in disbelief. "Do you remember who was saying that stuff?"

She waved her hand vaguely. "Just…people." She looked at me warily. "Skye? Are you okay?"

I was fuming. Who would say that about me, and why would anyone believe it? "How can people make such rude assumptions and then talk about them? It's my personal life! It's none of their business!"

Jenny hugged me. "I know. I was stupid to even listen. I'm sorry."

I shook my head and turned to open my locker. "How would you like it if they said things like that about you and Jon?" I asked, still burning.

"You're right," she said. "I'd be mad too."

I hung up my jacket and rummaged around in my locker, not really knowing what I was looking for. I stood up.

"Jenny," I said as casually as I could, "how long have you and Jon been going out now?"

"Four months," she said. "Remember? We started going out right after school got out last year."

I nodded. "You haven't, I mean…have you and Jon…you know…." I trailed off. I couldn't believe I was asking her this.

She started shaking her head before I even got to the "you know," and her cheeks were pink. "No," she said softly, "not yet."

I looked around to see if anyone was listening. "Not yet?"

Now her face was red. "I think we will soon. I…I didn't know how to talk to you about it."

"How soon is soon?" I asked.

She shifted from one foot to the other and looked down at her shoes. "His parents are going to be out of town this weekend." She glanced up at me. "I think it might be the right time."

I took a deep breath. "You need to *know* it's the right time," I reminded her. "Be sure, Jenny. You only get the first time once. Make sure you're really ready for it and that you're with the right guy. Remember, we both said we would wait at least a year, and make sure we were really in love."

She laughed, and I laughed with her. "I remember saying that. But sometimes when Jon holds me...." She shook her head ruefully. "I don't know if I want to wait. There have been a couple of times when we've come really close."

The bell rang.

"Oh, no!" I started pulling books from my locker.

"Skye, I've got to go all the way down to the science wing," she said.

"I know. I'll see you in English."

"'Kay," she said.

I found my Government book, shoved the other books back into my locker, and headed down the hall. "Hey there," Steve said, materializing at my side. "How are you doing today?"

"Fine," I said, managing a little grin. "How are you?" I couldn't help wondering if he had heard the rumors too.

"Okay. I'm just hoping that Phelps doesn't decide to collect the homework today. I didn't quite get it done."

"Maybe you could finish it up while he does roll," I suggested.

He grimaced. "Let me rephrase that. I haven't *started* the homework yet."

I laughed. Steve was one of the smartest guys in our class. He had at least three college prep classes, but he hardly ever did his homework. He floated along at a low B average. I was pretty sure my class would vote him "most likely to drop out of college and make a million dollars."

We split up at the door and headed to our assigned seats.

As I sat down, I saw that Steve had his head bent over his desk, scribbling furiously on a piece of notebook paper. I laughed to myself and chatted with the people who sat close to me till the bell rang. When Phelps announced that he was not going to collect homework today, I immediately looked over at Steve, who was looking at me. We shared a smile.

In the middle of class, Rosa, the girl to my left, handed me a note. I looked at it in surprise, because although my name was across the front of it, I didn't recognize the handwriting.

I held it in my lap and, when Phelps turned to write on the chalk-board, I opened the note and spread it out on the desk.

> Skye—
> I never did get a chance to ask you how your
> meet went on Thursday. I heard from a
> couple of your teammates that you dropped
> time. Congratulations! I look forward to seeing
> you swim in person. Just remember that the
> deal is that you come to a basketball game!
> Steve
> P.S. Looks like I got lucky with the homework!
> P.P.S. Want to go to a movie sometime?

I was grinning through the whole note, right up to the P.P.S., but when I got to the last line I suddenly felt my stomach drop to my toes. I automatically looked up at Steve. He grinned. I lowered my eyes in confusion. I couldn't tell how serious the note was. Maybe it was just a casual friend thing. He and I had had classes together since elementary school, but we had never seen each other outside of school. I didn't know what to do.

I pulled out a piece of notebook paper and wrote his name across the top. Then I just sat there for a long time. I decided to take the note as a casual friend thing, because I assumed he knew I was going out with Mike.

> Steve—
> Thank you! I did drop a little time on
> Thursday. Maybe you'll bring me good luck next
> week, and I'll drop enough time to go to
> state! And of course I'll come to a basket-
> ball game! I promised, didn't I? Oops, class
> is almost over. I'll see you sixth period!
> Skye

The bell rang a few minutes later, and as we all pushed our way out of the room, I handed Steve the note and then practically ran down the hall to American Lit class.

As soon as Jenny came into the room, I showed her the note from Steve. Her eyebrows climbed up her forehead.

"Whoa." She looked up at me. "Steve who?"

"Barker."

"Really?" She looked back down at the note. "Are you going to write him back?"

"I already did. I thanked him and told him I'd come to his game because I promised. Then I said class was over and I'd see him in art."

"You didn't say anything about the movie?"

I shook my head and shrugged at the same time. "No. I really didn't know how to answer that part."

"Probably good that you didn't. Wow, is Mike going to be jealous."

"Why?"

"Why? Because some cute guy is hitting on you, that's why!"

I shook my head again. "I really don't think he is. I think he's just trying to be friends."

Jenny looked at me in disbelief. "Skye, the guy is clearly asking you out!"

"Well, yeah, but…I mean…he's got to know about Mike and me, right? After all, it seems most people know more about us than I do!"

Jenny laughed. "Maybe you're right," she said, handing me the note. "But I still bet Mike gets really angry when you tell him."

"You mean *if* I tell him."

Jenny shook her head, her glossy black curls bouncing on her shoulders. "What do you mean, *if*?"

I chewed my bottom lip for a second. "Well, why should I tell him if he's just going to get mad?"

"Because he'll be really mad if he finds out from someone else!"

"Who'd tell him?" I asked pointedly.

"Well, I wouldn't." Her olive complexion darkened just a little. "So what are you going to do?"

I shrugged. "I already wrote him back. It's done."

Jenny grinned slyly at me. "You don't want it to be done."

"What do you mean?" I asked in an innocent tone.

"Admit it, Skye. He's cute."

"He's also nice to everyone," I added.

"See, I knew you were interested in him," said Jenny. "I can't believe this. Now you've got two cute guys after you."

The bell rang, and Jenny scooted quickly back over to her chair. I had a hard time listening to the lecture on the story we had just read. I kept thinking about Mike and Steve. Steve made the whole class laugh whenever he wanted. Mike dominated the hallway just by walking down it. Steve was bright without trying. Mike studied hard just to stay eligible. I was attracted to both of them, but it was Mike who made my stomach flutter. I had to admit, though, that I wasn't sure whether it fluttered because I liked him so much or because I was so nervous around him.

The rest of the day passed quickly, and before I knew it, it was time for art class. Jenny and I shared a table, and Steve sat two tables back and one row over. I was a little nervous going into the classroom, afraid that there would be a note waiting for me on my desk or something. There wasn't.

When Steve came in, he said hi, and then went on back to his seat. That was all. I was relieved, and exchanged a smile with Jenny, because that showed I had been right—he was just interested in friendship. But a small part of me was almost disappointed.

⁓

On Tuesday, I was so excited about driving the car to school that I actually made Sunny get up early. I don't know what I was thinking. We got to school so early, we were the tenth car in the parking lot. Not a single person I knew saw me pull up.

The day went really well, except that I didn't see Mike at all. I wasn't too worried about it, because I knew I'd see him later, when I went to pick him up for dinner.

Sunny met me by my locker right after school, just as I had told him to. In fact, he was waiting for me when I got there. He was bouncing from one foot to the other.

Jenny smiled at him. "You look like you had a good day, Sunny."

He shrugged, but couldn't quit grinning. "It was okay."

"You seem awfully excited about an okay day," Jenny said, opening her locker.

"Skye's going to teach me how to swim this afternoon," he said, and he actually jumped up in the air.

Jenny tilted her head toward me. "You didn't tell me about that," she said.

I shook my head ever so slightly. "I'll call and tell you about it tonight. Good luck at your meet. You're doing your new dismount tonight, right?"

"Yeah," she said, smiling and shutting her locker.

"Did you get your Lit book?" I asked.

"Ugh! No, of course not." Shaking her head and muttering to herself, she dropped her book bag on the floor and began twirling the combination lock again.

I laughed and picked up my bag. It was great to have only one bag to carry, since I had been able to leave my swimming gear in the car. I had tried to get Sunny to do the same thing, but he had insisted on bringing his bag inside with him. I didn't ask, but I was pretty sure he had carried his swimming bag to all of his classes with him. I couldn't remember ever being that excited to swim.

We walked out to the car and I drove us over to the community center. Getting in and out of the parking lot took almost as long as walking. I stopped Sunny just as he started to get out of the car.

"Come on, Skye, let's go!"

"Sunny, I need you to listen to me very carefully." He was looking out the window. "Put your bag down and look at me," I commanded.

Reluctantly he turned to look at me.

"Now," I said slowly. "You need to pay attention and remember this. I'm not going to teach you your lessons."

His face got red almost instantly, and his eyes filled with tears. "You promithed!" he yelled. "You told Mom I wath going to have my lethon today!"

"Sunny, listen to me," I said patiently. "I'm not done yet. You are going to have your first lesson tonight. I'm just not going to be your teacher, that's all."

"What do you mean?"

"You know Sandra, the lifeguard?"

"Yeah," he said slowly.

"She's going to teach your class on Tuesdays and Thursdays, and Rob is going to teach your class on Saturday mornings."

He frowned at me, and his eyes showed his confusion. "But I want you to be my teacher. Why can't you teach me?"

"Because, Sunny, after practice I'm too tired to stay in the pool. And if I'm tired, I'm also grumpy. You know that." He smiled a little for me. "So this way, I won't be grumpy, and you can still learn how to swim."

He sat there for a moment, thinking. "Okay," he said. "Can we go in now?"

"No," I said, shaking my head. "There's one more thing."

"What?"

"You can never tell Mom that I'm not teaching you. You always have to tell her that I'm your teacher."

"But that's lying," he said doubtfully.

"Yes," I said slowly. "But if you want to learn how to swim, then you have to tell this one little lie."

He looked at me and didn't say anything.

"Sunny, if you ever tell Mom that I'm not teaching your lessons, I'll never talk to you again. I'll never help you again," I said slowly, letting him know I was serious. "I'll never be able to trust you again."

His face turned pale.

"I'm telling you the truth, Sunny. Do you believe me?"

He nodded, his eyes wide.

"Good. Can you keep this one secret?"

He nodded again.

"Great!" I smiled at him. "Then let's get going!"

I had a good time at practice that night. Knowing that I was going to be out with Mike without Sunny made everything seem wonderful. I joked around with Hannah, and we both tried to mutiny on Coach when he gave us a hard set. We splashed him when he gave it to us, so he got mad and doubled it. I was so happy, I didn't even care.

I think I took the world's fastest shower in the locker room. I was halfway out the door to the car when I realized that I should check on Sunny and make sure he knew what was going on before I left.

When I got back out on the pool deck, it only took me a couple of minutes to find Sandra. Sunny was with her, and the rest of his class. They were all lined up alongside the pool, listening to Sandra's directions. Sunny towered over the other kids, most of whom were only six or seven years old. The others were giggling nervously, but Sunny was staring at the water. I went over to Sandra real quick and told her I'd be back in forty-five minutes to pick Sunny up. Then I waved to him and ran out to the car.

~

I rang the doorbell to Mike's house, then smoothed my hair, trying to calm down. I felt all giddy inside.

He opened the door and swept me into a big embrace without saying a word. He picked me up and carried me inside and down the stairs. Every time I tried to say something, he stopped me with a kiss.

In his bedroom, he set me down on the edge of his bed and locked his lips on mine. At first I couldn't get the rumors from school out of my mind, but when he kept kissing me, I forgot about everything else. His hands started roving everywhere. Nervously, I let my hands do some roving of their own. I didn't really know what I was doing. I was terrified I'd do something wrong and he'd laugh at me. I just knew I loved the way his chest felt, and his shoulders, and his back. I tried to pull away a little, but he just drew me closer.

Somehow, again, his hand ended up inside my shirt. He was tracing up and down my back lightly, then my side, back to my back, back to my side but a little more toward the front, then to my back again. I tried to enjoy this new tingling feeling, but I was too nervous and scared to relax. I was terrified his parents would walk in at any moment.

Finally, I pushed him away to get some air. "Wow," I gasped. "That was a really nice hello."

He grinned. "I'm not done saying hello yet," he said, bending his head down again.

I turned my head. "We'd better get going."

"Where?" he murmured into my hair.

"To get something to eat."

"I've got all I want to nibble on right here."

I laughed. "Mike, I'm hungry. Come on." I stood up and started edging toward the door. "Let's go say hi to your parents and go to McDonald's or Taco Bell. I've only got a little over half an hour before I need to head back to the pool."

"My parents aren't here," he said softly. "They went out to a movie. A half hour's plenty of time. Let's just stay here." He started to move toward me again.

I back-pedaled quickly out of his room and into the hall. "Mike," I said. "I really need something to eat!"

He sighed. "Okay. How about we go get you something to eat and then we bring it back here?"

"Please, Mike?" I said. "We don't have much time. I just want to go eat dinner with my boyfriend, okay?"

He groaned. "Yeah, okay." He grabbed his coat and climbed the stairs to the front door. I followed him.

He was quiet on the drive to McDonald's. I ordered, but he said he didn't want anything.

"Is this for here or to go?" the girl behind the counter asked.

"Here," I said, at the same time Mike said, "To go."

"Which one?" the girl asked, looking back and forth at us.

"Here," I said, looking at Mike.

He shook his head and walked away from the counter. I paid for my dinner, a regular hamburger and small fries. I reminded myself to buy something for Sunny before I left, to help convince him to keep our secret.

I found Mike in the very back corner, at a table with chairs. I looked at him and then looked over at the booth. I set the tray on the booth's table and slid in.

"Why don't you come sit over here?" I asked, patting the seat next to me. "We could cuddle over here."

He just stared at me for a moment. "You won't stay at my house and cuddle, but you want me to cuddle at McDonald's?"

I looked down at my fries, trying to hide my disappointment and embarrassment. "You didn't want to just cuddle at your house and you know it."

I heard him get up. He slid into the booth across from me. "Yeah, I know. Is that so wrong? Come on, Skye, we've been dating for a long time now."

"Not even a month!"

"So? Lots of people have already done it. Most guys I know wouldn't have waited this long."

I was stunned. "Then why don't you go date *their* girlfriends?" I snapped. I felt like I was choking on a french fry.

He sighed. "I don't want to be with them, I want to be with you."

"Then you'll wait."

He got up again, stepped around the table, and slid onto the seat next to me. "Yeah, I guess I will." He reached out and took a fry.

"I thought you said you didn't want any."

"I changed my mind." He looked at me. "And I hope you'll tell me you've changed your mind soon."

"Believe me, you'll be the first to know."

He grinned. "Good."

We sat in silence for a few minutes. I wanted to ask him if he had heard the rumors, but I didn't know how to bring it up.

"So," he said finally, "what color is your homecoming dress going to be?"

I shrugged, trying not to show my excitement. I had never been to a homecoming dance. "I haven't even thought about it." I looked up at him through my eyelashes. "It's not good to think about buying a dress for a dance when you haven't even been asked yet."

He looked at me funny, and I could see that it took a few seconds for my point to sink in. Then he grinned. He took my hand, and then backed off the booth, pulling me so I ended up just at the edge of the seat. He knelt down on one knee.

"Oh, dear, beautiful, brilliant Skye, wiltst thou goest to thine home-coming dance withith mine?"

I burst out laughing. "Your Shakespeare needs some work," I said, catching my breath.

He dropped my hand and put his hands on his hips. "I give you a romantic proposal, and all you can tell me is that my Shakespeare needs work?" he demanded.

I took a deep breath and tried to get a serious expression on my face. "Oh, Michael mine, I would be proud to have thee as mine escort to the fair homecoming dance."

He was sulking. "I'm not sure I want to go with someone who speaks Shakespeare better than me."

I couldn't resist. "Better than I," I corrected, giggling.

"See? Why would I want to spend my evening with a bookworm like you?"

I reached out, grabbed his hand, and pulled it up close to my face. "Because," I murmured, kissing his first, second, and then third fingers, "mine heart belongs to thee." I kissed his pinkie and then the back of his hand.

He looked at me. "Is that a yes?"

I laughed. "Yes."

"Good," he said, standing up and scooting me over in the booth so he could sit down next to me. "So what color dress are you wearing?"

"I told you I don't know yet."

"When will you know?"

I shrugged. "Probably in a couple of weeks."

"You'll tell me at least a week before the dance? I'll need to get a matching corsage."

"Sure," I said, nodding. I looked at my watch. "We better get going," I said.

"Okay," he said, sliding back out of the booth. "What does Sunny want?"

"I'm sure he'd like a Happy Meal, but I can get it."

He turned and walked around the corner. By the time I had thrown my trash away, he was already at the counter. I heard him ask for a Happy Meal. And then he pulled out his wallet.

"Mike!" I hissed behind him. He turned to glance at me. "I said I was going to get it!"

He just shook his head as the girl behind the counter gave him his change.

I was absurdly touched. "You don't have to do this," I said.

"No," he agreed, "I don't. Just make sure your brother knows that I did. Maybe it'll make him like me."

I hugged him from behind. "You're the best."

"Make sure you remember that," he said, patting my hand.

We walked out of the McDonald's, and I opened the car door for him with a smile. Then I went around to the driver's side.

"So what are you doing Saturday?" I asked.

"Don't know. Why?"

"Sunny has a lesson in the morning, but I get the car all day."

He grinned. "I think somebody wants to get out of the house."

I grinned back. "I was thinking of going to the mall and then catching an afternoon movie."

"I think I could go for that," he said easily. "Is this a private date, or are we inviting other friends?"

"Let's invite Jenny and Jon," I said quickly. It wouldn't be a private date anyway; Sunny would be with us. I didn't mention that, though.

I drove Mike home and dropped him off, then hurried back over to the pool. I was about ten minutes late. I'd been planning to get back in time to see the last five minutes of the lesson.

Sunny was dressed and waiting for me when I got there. He didn't look happy.

"Hey!" I said, smiling brightly. "Did you already shower and everything?"

He gave a curt nod.

"Did you have fun?"

Another nod.

I held out the Happy Meal box. "I brought you McDonald's." He didn't move, so I took a step closer to him. "It'd be a good idea if you ate it here." I didn't want Mom finding it in the trash and asking questions. On school nights I wasn't allowed to go anywhere but practice or home.

"I'm not hungry." He was in a full-blown pout.

"This is all you get for dinner, Sunny," I said. "Either you eat this here and now, or you're not going to be eating till tomorrow morning."

He dropped his bag and grabbed the box out of my hand. Then he sat down on the floor right there in the lobby.

Sandra came out of the guards' locker room. "Hey, Sunny!" She smiled at him. "You did a great job today."

"Thanks." He gave her a great big smile, and then, to make sure his point was clear, he glared at me again before he went back to the hamburger.

I ignored his glare. "What all did you do today?" I asked Sandra.

"We did bobs, practiced blowing bubbles, and tried back and front floats. Sunny can do it all."

"Cool!" I smiled at Sunny, but he kept his eyes on the hamburger.

"He did great for his first lesson," she said. She hesitated, then added in a lower voice, "I don't think he's real happy about being so much older than the rest of the class, but he's doing fine. He should probably be in a level three class, but we don't offer those until eight."

"That's too late," I said.

Sunny had finished his hamburger. He got up and threw the box away and then turned to me. "I want to go home."

"Okay. See ya, Sandra," I said. "And thanks for everything."

"Bye, Skye. See you on Thursday, Sunny!"

He barely waved to her on his way out the door.

I caught up to him at the car. "What's your problem?" I demanded. "You had no right to be that rude to Sandra."

"I want to go home," he said again. He stuck his out lower lip and waited for me to open the car door. I crossed my arms over my chest, waiting.

I don't know how long we stood there in the cold, dark parking lot. I was so focused on his stupid lower lip with the steam coming out of his mouth, that it took me a few minutes to realize he was crying. I threw my hands up in the air.

"*What?* What is your problem? You got your swimming lesson, Sandra says you're doing well, I brought you McDonald's. So what? What is so wrong? You got everything you wanted, and you're still crying."

"I want to go home," he repeated.

"You've gotten everything else you want tonight. Don't worry, you'll get that too," I fumed. "But right now you have to do what *I* want. You have to tell me why you're crying."

He turned around and started walking home.

"Abraham Walter, don't you dare turn your back on me!" I screamed at him.

"Then take me home!" he yelled back.

"No!" I watched him walk away, knowing I was in huge trouble if Mom found out about any of this. But I was so sick of him always getting his way! I climbed into the car and started it, so the heater would get going.

I sat there in the idling car and watched as Sunny walked all the way down the block and then made the first turn. I turned on the lights, put the car in gear, and followed him. I stopped at the top of the street, deciding to wait there till he made the next turn on the way home. Instead, he turned into the elementary school.

"Great," I muttered to myself. "I really don't need this."

I put the car in gear again and pulled into the school parking lot. By the time I turned the lights off, Sunny was sitting in one of the swings. The parking lot light showed his silhouette. He was the picture of utter dejection. His head was bowed down, his back and shoulders were slumped forward, and his toes were barely dragging along the ground as the swing swayed ever so slightly.

I pushed myself out of the car and walked slowly down the hill to the swings. He didn't look up as I sat down in the swing next to him.

After a few moments, I said, "This was more fun the last time we were here."

He didn't answer.

"Come on, Sunny," I pleaded. "Would you please tell me what's so wrong?"

He was shaking his head slowly.

"Didn't you have fun with your lessons?" I asked.

"I hate them!"

"See, I tried to tell you that you didn't want to swim," I said smugly.

"No!" he almost shouted. "I like thwimming. I hate the lethons!"

"Why?"

"They're baby lethons! They're just little kidth." He seemed to be calming down a little. "It's stupid. I hate it."

"Sunny, that's just because it's level one, for beginners. It's mostly little kids who take that level. There's nothing wrong with being older than the rest of them."

"I'm *always* older than everyone."

I winced. What he'd said was true. He was a year and a half older than me, but we were in the same grade. I had never thought of it bothering him. In fact, I usually forgot he was my older brother. I know I treat him like a little brother; I always have. Even though his occupational therapist said he was capable of doing things on his own, it was easier to do things for him instead of watching his slow struggle.

"Sunny," I began.

"That's why I wanted you to teach me," he interrupted. "So I wouldn't have to be with the little kids."

My heart sank. "Sunny, look, I'm sorry, okay? I wasn't thinking. But I've already paid for the lessons. It's just six weeks. And then swim season will almost be over, and I can start teaching you. Just you and me, okay?"

His head was still down. "Where were you?"

"Huh?"

"Where were you while I was swimming?"

"You know where I was. I went to get you McDonald's."

"You were gone the whole time."

"I'm sorry. I tried to get back in time to see the end of the lesson. I will next time, okay?"

"You were with Mike, weren't you?"

My stomach tightened. "Yes, I was." Before he could say something else, I continued, "And he paid for your dinner. He's trying to be your friend."

He didn't say anything, so we just sat in silence.

Finally I sighed. "Look, Sunny, all I can say is that I'm sorry all the other kids in your swimming class are so little. But I've already paid for the lessons. I'll teach you when this session is over. I brought you McDonald's. And I'll take you to a movie this weekend. That's the best I can do."

"Will you take me home now?"

"Will you tell Mom?" I countered.

"No."

"Then I'll take you home. And I'll make you hot chocolate when we get there," I added.

"Okay," he said listlessly.

"Are you sure it's okay?" I asked.

"Yeah."

"And you won't tell Mom?" I pressed.

"No. I won't tell."

"Thanks, Sunny."

We got up and went back to the car in silence, the distance between us growing with each step.

～

I didn't see much of Mike the rest of that week. That made Sunny happy, but I was counting the hours till Saturday.

On Thursday, the junior varsity had an away scrimmage. The whole team went because Coach Sullivan believes in team unity. I was disappointed when I didn't get to see Mike all day, because I wore my miniskirt just for him.

Usually I enjoy being at meets when I'm not swimming, because it gives me more time to talk to people and I don't get stressed. On Thursday, though, all I wanted to do was get back to our pool and then go see Mike.

I barely got Sunny back to his lesson on time, and then I went right over to Mike's house. Even though I was in a hurry, I made sure I was under the speed limit. I couldn't afford to get a ticket, especially not during the time I was supposed to be teaching Sunny.

When I got to Mike's house, a note was taped to the door. Mike's parents had taken him out for dinner, and no one was home. I was disappointed, but at least he had remembered to leave me a note.

I couldn't wait for Saturday.

CHAPTER SEVEN

H ey, Mom?" I called softly into the bathroom.

She opened the door, drying her hair with a towel. "What are you doing up? Did you forget what day it is?" she asked. The office where Mom worked was open on Saturdays, and she usually had to go in.

"I wanted to catch you before you left. Can I get my allowance for next week?"

"What happened to the money I gave you just the other day?" she asked.

"I already spent it."

"On what?"

"Lunches, and I bought Jenny a shirt for her birthday."

"Oh." She paused. "Can't you wait till next week?"

"Please, Mom. I want to take Sunny to a movie after swimming today."

She looked at me for a moment. I tried to look as miserable and innocent as I could. Finally she sighed. "All right, I'll leave you ten more on the counter before I leave."

I made a face.

"What?" she snapped irritably.

"Nothing," I said instantly, backing off. I had gotten as much out of her as I could, and reminding her how much movie tickets cost, even for the matinee shows, wasn't going to improve her mood any. I would just have to hope Sunny had some extra money socked away.

Instead of going back to bed as I had planned, I went into the kitchen. I put the last two pieces of bread into the toaster, then added bread to the list that was stuck to the fridge. I nuked a mug of water in the microwave for a minute, and then put butter and grape jam on the toast. I dropped the tea bag into the mug and was just picking everything up to take to Mom when she came into the kitchen. Her eyebrow went up.

"Now what are you doing?"

"Making you breakfast."

"Why?" she asked suspiciously.

"Because breakfast is the most important meal of the day, and you never have time to eat it."

"And?"

"And nothing. That's it."

"You sure you're not going to hit me up for more money now?"

I shook my head. "This is my thank-you for the ten." I said simply.

She kind of cocked her head to one side to look at me, and I could tell she didn't believe me.

"I'm serious," I said, "and I'm tired, so now I'm going back to bed. Have a good day."

I was halfway down the hall before she finally said, "Thanks, Skye."

When I got up again a couple hours later, there was a note waiting for me taped to the fridge:

> Skye—
> Thank you for breakfast this morning. Have fun at the movies!
> Love,
> Mom

A twenty was folded up inside the note.

"All right, Mom!"

~

"Here, Skye, this is your color," Jenny sang out across the store.

I turned and stared in disbelief at the ugliest dress I had ever seen. It was a split-pea soup kind of green, trimmed with bright orange paisley print, and the bottom of the dress had a yellow fringe that looked like it had come off some really old bedspread. She turned it ever so slightly in the light, and I saw that there were also rhinestones worked into the collar and sleeves.

I gave her my biggest grin and then turned to Mike, beaming. "That's the dress I'm wearing to homecoming!" I gushed, leading him over to Jenny. "I haven't found a more perfect dress anywhere."

He grimaced and shook himself as if he had been dipped in some really nasty slime. "Ugh. You put that on, and you're going to dance alone."

"Oh, Mike, you mean you don't like me no matter how I look?" I pouted, taking the dress from Jenny and holding it up to myself. I looked at the price tag. "Yow! This has got to be a joke." I showed the tag to Jen. "Who in their right mind would pay that much for this thing?" I demanded.

"Who in their right mind would pay anything for it?" Jenny countered.

We were both laughing.

"I don't know," Jon said, tilting his head to look at the dress. "I might pay a couple bucks for it."

"What for?" Jenny asked.

"It would make a great Halloween costume. You could go as some sort of sociopath."

We were all laughing a little too loudly. The salesclerk who had already asked us three times if we needed any help was giving us a dirty look. I hung the awful green dress back on the rack and flipped through the other dresses in my size. A blue sheath with a low-cut back caught my eye. I pulled it out and held it up to me, but I was afraid to look at the price tag.

"Skye?" Sunny said. "We need to go. The movie starts soon."

I looked over my shoulder. Sunny had been doing such a good job of just staying behind us and being invisible that for a moment I had forgotten he was there.

"No problem, Sunny," Mike said, waving a hand at him. "We've got plenty of time."

Sunny didn't say anything. He just pleaded with his eyes. I hung the dress back on the rack.

"You're right, Sunny, we should get going." I grabbed Mike's hand and said in a low-pitched voice, "Sunny likes to get there early so he can get a seat in the center."

Mike shrugged. "Whatever."

We walked out of the store and headed toward the theater. Jenny and Jon had their arms around each other and were walking in front of Mike and me, and Sunny trailed a few feet behind us. Mike and I were holding hands and swinging them back and forth lazily. Jenny stopped at almost every window and made a comment about something. We were all laughing and having a great time. Sunny was quiet.

"Mike!" a voice shouted suddenly.

We all turned around. Three girls were headed toward us. One of them was DeAnna Garcia, the girl who had broken up with Mike at the end of the summer. I didn't really know her, but at that moment, I hated her.

"You didn't return my call," she said, managing to smile and pout at the same time.

"Sorry, Dee," Mike said with easy familiarity.

I moved over closer to Mike, making sure she could see me.

"What are you doing here?" she asked, ignoring me.

"We're going to see a movie," I said quickly.

DeAnna didn't even flick her eyes toward me. "What are you doing later tonight?"

"I don't know," Mike said. "What's up?"

"Oh, I just know of a really good party that's going on. Give me a call if you're interested," she said as she turned away. The other two girls were laughing. "Buh-bye," she called.

"Bye," Mike said, smiling after them.

"Ahem." I cleared my throat loudly.

Mike glanced down at me. "You can't go out tonight, can you?"

"No," I said, trying to keep my voice steady. I wasn't going to let DeAnna ruin the day for me.

"Didn't think so. Come on, let's get going."

We finally reached the movie theater. We stood as a group, with Sunny hanging back just a little, looking at the marquee. *The DragonMaster* started at 2:10. It was five till two.

"See?" Mike said, turning to Sunny. "I told you we would make it in plenty of time."

"The movie starts in five minutes," Sunny said. "Let's go."

Mike dropped his voice and muttered something. I couldn't hear it, but Jon began to laugh.

I shook my head at Sunny. "The movie doesn't start for another fifteen minutes."

Sunny's eyes got wide and he shook his head forcefully. He pointed up to the marquee. "It says it starts at two."

I followed his finger and then grinned. "We're seeing *The DragonMaster,* Sunny. Look at the next line."

"But I don't want to thee that movie!" he cried out. He looked like he was on the verge of tears.

I dropped Mike's hand and took a few slow steps toward Sunny. He stepped back with every step I took forward. "Why not?" I asked, careful to keep my voice low and calm. He had been looking pale and panicky all day. I didn't want to push him over the edge.

"It lookth thcary," he said.

Mike snorted. "It's supposed to be," he said.

"What do you want to see, Sunny?" I asked him, ignoring Mike.

"That one," he said, pointing at a poster. *Somebody Save Scamp!* was the title, and the poster showed a goofy-looking animated dog in the middle of a huge mess of cats and overturned fishbowls.

"What a baby!" Mike exclaimed.

"Sunny," I sighed, pretending I didn't hear Mike's comment, "we don't want to see a cartoon."

"Well, I don't want to thee the other one." He pouted, crossing his arms over his chest.

I put my hands over my face and took a deep breath. Then I pulled my hands down and looked at him. "Can you handle seeing a movie by yourself?" I asked him very seriously.

He looked at me for a minute, and I knew he was honestly thinking about it before he answered. "Yeth," he said finally.

"Okay, come on." I walked him up to the ticket booth and got him a ticket. Then I turned to him. "Our movie will last a little longer than yours. I need you to promise me you'll wait right there." I pointed to a bench a few feet away. "Stay there until we come out."

His head bobbed up and down. "Okay."

"You sure you can handle this?" I asked again. Any other day I would have been happy to see him trying to go to the movie by himself. Today I was worried because he had been so quiet and moody. He still looked kind of pale.

He gave me a quick grin. "I'll be okay." He turned and walked into the theater lobby.

I watched till he disappeared down the hall to the individual theaters, and was about to turn around when Jenny came and grabbed me from behind. I just barely bit back a scream.

"Come on," she whispered into my ear. "Come with me to the bathroom."

She dragged me off to the mall restrooms before I had a chance to protest.

"Jenny!" I exclaimed as the bathroom door shut behind us. "What's going on?"

"We need to talk," she said, leaning against the wall.

"Okay," I said. "About what?"

"Mike and Jon are talking about skipping the movie and coming back to pick up Sunny later."

"What would we do?" I asked.

"Go to Jon's house."

When I didn't say anything right away, she added, "His parents are out of town this weekend, remember?"

I nodded. "I remember."

She sighed. "Look, Skye, I just thought we should decide what we want to do together, before we get out there and someone gets talked into doing something they don't want to."

"You mean me," I said dully.

She gave a half-shrug. "I don't know. I might mean me, too. I'm not really sure I want to know there's another couple in another room doing the same thing at the same time, you know what I mean?"

"I think it would be too weird," I said.

She nodded. "Me too." We smiled at each other.

Impulsively I hugged her. "I knew you were my best friend for a reason."

She laughed. "Only one reason?"

I laughed, too, but then I got serious again. "We should probably just tell them that we can't leave Sunny alone."

Nodding, she said, "That's kind of what I was thinking, too. That way they won't get all snotty about it."

"Okay." We both took a deep breath at the same time.

"Ready?" she asked.

I started to nod, but then I shook my head. She let me stand there for a moment, not saying anything.

"Am I just being stupid?" I finally asked her, staring at my feet. "I mean, it's no big deal, right? Everyone else is doing it."

Jenny was shaking her head. "I'm the wrong one to be asking. I haven't done it yet either, remember? And," she said, taking another deep breath, "for me it *is* a big deal. There's too much at stake for it not to be a big deal."

I nodded. We had heard all the lectures on AIDS, STDs, and teen pregnancy. And Mom had gone on for quite a while about the emotional impact of having sex when she had given me "the talk."

Jenny added, "And just because other people don't think it's a big deal shouldn't really matter, I guess."

I nodded. "I'm afraid Mike will break up with me if I don't agree soon."

"Then he's not worth it," Jenny said flatly. "Jon and I have been going together longer than the two of you have, and Jon isn't putting nearly as much pressure on me as it seems Mike is on you."

"Is Jon putting pressure on you too?" I asked, glancing up at her.

Jenny shrugged. "Kind of. A little. Well, no, not really." She smiled at me. "No more pressure than I'm putting on myself." Laughing self-consciously, she added, "I really like him, Skye, and the way he makes me feel sometimes…" Her words trailed off.

"I think I know what you mean," I said. I hesitated before I asked her, "Does Jon ever scare you?"

"What do you mean?"

"Like you say no, or stop, and he keeps going? Like you're afraid that maybe some time he won't stop, no matter what you say?"

Jenny frowned. "No. I never feel like that." She took a long look at me. "You don't think Mike would ever—"

"Forget it. Maybe I'm just being stupid. I mean, he's always stopped."

"So far," she said.

Suddenly the conversation was making me uneasy. "Come on. They're going to think we've ditched them or something."

She stopped me. "Let's just get this clear. We're going to stay and watch the movie, right?"

"Right."

"And if Mike ever gets out of line, you'll tell me, right? After you kick his butt and dump him on it?"

"Right."

"Okay, let's go."

Mike and Jon were still standing where we had left them, but even from a distance I could see the tension in Mike's face. Jenny immediately went up to Jon and gave him a kiss, then stood with her arm wrapped around him. I couldn't see, but I was willing to bet that she had her hand in his back pocket.

"Hey," Mike said, "sometime you're going to have to tell us why girls always go to the bathroom together."

I shook my head and grinned. "Can't reveal gender secrets. It's a law."

He laughed, but it was a half-hearted laugh. "Well, let's get going."

"Okay," I said, and turned to the theater box office.

"No, no, Skye. Jon and I have decided we should skip the movie."

I raised my eyebrows. "So what are you and Jon going to do?"

"We're going to Jon's house."

"Okay, have fun," I said. "Come on, Jenny."

"Okay," Jenny said, stepping away from Jon.

Mike was shaking his head, smiling confidently. "No, no. You're coming with us."

"We are?" I looked at Jenny. "I don't remember making that decision. Do you?"

"I sure don't," Jenny said.

"Come on, we can catch the movie some other time," Mike said.

"So what are we going to do now that we couldn't do at some other time?" I asked him, looking him straight in the eye.

Mike got just a little pink. "Jon's parents are out of town," was all he said.

I didn't say anything. We all just stood there looking at each other for a few moments. It was extremely uncomfortable.

"Look," Jenny said finally. "The movie's about to start."

Mike hadn't taken his eyes off mine. I felt like he was trying to bore a hole into my head. "I don't want to see the movie," he said.

"I don't want to go to Jon's," I countered, abandoning the plan to blame everything on Sunny.

"Why not?"

"Because you're trying to make all these decisions about me without asking what I want," I said angrily. "I want to go see the movie."

"We can do that later."

"We can have sex later, too," I said bluntly. "We're not going to now."

Jenny and Jon were looking everywhere but at us.

"I don't think you'll ever say yes."

"That's a definite possibility," I agreed. I was so angry. I didn't want my first time to be just sex anyway. I wanted it to be romantic. I wanted it to be making love. But I couldn't say any of those things to Mike. He obviously wouldn't understand.

"I'm going to the movie. You all can go do what you want to do."

I turned and walked up to the ticket booth. I pushed my money through the little window. "One, please, for *The DragonMaster.*"

When I turned around, Jenny was right behind me, but Jon and Mike were gone. Jenny's face was red and her jaw was clenched.

"One please," she clipped out as she shoved her money through the window.

Neither of us said anything until we were seated in the dark theater. The previews had already started.

"I can't believe them!" she whispered loudly. "They weren't even going to ask us what we wanted to do!"

"I know. It really ticks me off."

"Me too." She kind of giggled. "You let Mike have it, though. I was so proud of you. I'm not sure I could have said it like that, all cold and angry."

"Did I sound cold? 'Cause it felt like my face was on fire. Did Jon leave too?"

"Yeah. I told him that he should go with Mike."

The previews ended, and we stopped talking. I had a hard time focusing on the movie. I was still really angry. My feet were tapping. I couldn't sit still. I was so angry, I felt sick to my stomach.

The queasy feeling didn't go away. Finally I leaned over to Jenny. "Be right back," I whispered. "I've got to go to the bathroom."

I walked quickly up the aisle and out the door.

I was halfway to the bathroom when I noticed a group of theater workers in a huddle in the center of the lobby. I slowed my pace a little out of curiosity. When I heard crying coming from the center of the huddle, I stopped. I'd recognize those huge, ripping sobs anywhere.

"Sunny?" I started toward the huddle. The people with their backs to me turned and opened the circle, revealing a miserable figure in the center. Sunny's red face was streaked with tears, and his breath came in great hitches. He saw me and lurched forward, almost falling on me. He wrapped me in a great bear hug and buried his face in my shoulder, still sobbing.

"Do you know him?" an older balding guy, probably the theater manager, asked me.

"Yeah," I said. "Sunny, what's wrong?"

"Do you know how we can reach his family?" the old guy continued.

"I'm his sister," I said. Some of the theater employees began to move away. "What happened?"

"I don't know," the guy said. "He became hysterical in the theater."

"Sunny?" His sobbing had abated a little, but he still had a grip on me that I couldn't break.

"I'm not so sure it's a good idea for him to see a movie alone," the balding guy said, looking at me.

I just nodded. I didn't know what to do.

"Do you have a way to take him home?" he asked.

"Yeah, no, I mean…yeah, I have a way to get him home, but my friend and I just paid for tickets to a different movie."

The manager started to open his mouth, and I was pretty sure he was going to say there wouldn't be any refund because it wasn't the theater's fault. Just then, Sunny let out a great quivering sigh that shook both of us. "Under the circumstances, we'll be happy to refund your money," the manager said.

I nodded over Sunny's head to him.

"Yes, well, um…." The bald guy was beginning to look as lost as I was feeling. "I'll leave you two now."

Slowly I was able to lead Sunny over to the bench at the side of the lobby and coax him into sitting down.

"Sunny, what happened?" I foolishly asked again. His eyes began to fill again and his lip began to quiver. "Okay, okay, never mind," I said quickly. "It doesn't matter anyway."

I waited a few minutes while he calmed himself down again. "I need to go get Jenny, okay?"

He just stared at me.

"I'll be right back, okay?" I slowly eased myself off the bench. He reached up and grabbed frantically at my hand. I caught his hand and gently pushed it back. "I'll be right back, Sunny. I promise. Just wait right here. I'll be back before you can count to one hundred."

"Promith?" He sniffled.

"Promise," I sighed back.

I went in and whispered quickly to Jenny. "I've got to take Sunny home right now."

She made a face, but didn't say anything. Instead she nodded, stood up, and followed me out of the theater.

I was glad I had driven instead of Mike, or we wouldn't have a way home.

The bald guy was standing next to Sunny when we got out to the lobby. He didn't say anything, just handed me the refund and then walked off. I gave Jenny her money.

"Okay, Sunny, let's go."

"Where're Mike and Jon?" he asked, looking around.

"Something came up, so they had to go home," I said. Sunny didn't need to know about the fight.

"Oh," Sunny said as he stood up.

When we turned to walk out of the mall, Sunny grabbed my hand. He kept it in a tight grip the entire way out to the car, and he walked so close to me he stepped on my foot several times. None of us talked. It took me a full minute to convince Sunny to let go of my hand when we got to the car.

As I started the engine, I turned to Jenny. "Want to come over and hang out at my house for a while?"

She shook her head. "Thanks, but I think I'd rather just go home now."

"Okay." I nodded. I wasn't really sure if I felt like having her over or not anyway. I turned on the radio and we barely spoke on the way to her house.

"I'll call you tonight," Jenny said as she climbed out of the car.

"If you don't, I'll call you."

"Sunny, do you want to move to the front?" Jenny asked.

He shook his head.

I gave an angry laugh. "He knows if he gets close to me, I might kill him before we get home."

Jenny smiled, but it was a strained smile. "Don't be mad at him, Skye. I'm not sure I could have stayed for the rest of the movie anyway."

I nodded. "I know. Me neither."

We waved good-bye and I waited till she disappeared into her front door before I pulled out.

Sunny was quiet for the rest of the ride, and as soon as we got home he ran to the bathroom. Even though he pulled the door shut behind him, I could hear him throwing up.

I went to the kitchen to get him some Sprite, but mostly to get away from the bathroom. I didn't feel so great myself. Just listening to someone get sick always makes me want to throw up too.

Before I took the soda to him, I stopped and just stood still for a few minutes, resting my head against the cool refrigerator door. I was having a bad day anyway, and now I would have to spend the rest of it taking care of a sick brother. Of course, I should have recognized that he was getting sick. Sunny always gets real quiet and emotional when he's coming down with something.

By the time I got back down the hall, Sunny was already curled up on his bed with his head buried in the pillows.

I knocked lightly on the open door as I went in. "Want some Sprite?"

"Uh-uh." He shook his head.

"How about I just leave it here in case you change your mind?" I said, setting the glass on the bookshelf by his bed. "What's wrong? Is it just your stomach?"

He shook his head again. "I have a headache too," he whispered.

"When did you start feeling this way?"

"Last night."

"Sunny," I groaned. "Why didn't you just tell me?"

"I didn't want to miss my lesson," he said.

I sighed. "First off, swimming this morning probably made it worse. Second, even if it didn't make it worse, now you've probably given whatever it is you have to your entire class, and the teacher."

He looked at me. "Do you think I gave it to you and Jenny?"

"I don't know. Maybe. And Mike and Jon too."

I could tell by the look on his face that he didn't care about Mike and Jon.

"You look tired," I told him.

He nodded.

"I'll go get you some Tylenol. Then you should try to take a nap."

"Okay," he said.

I took Sunny his Tylenol, then tinkered around the house for a while. I sat and flipped through all the TV stations a couple of times, then turned it off. I tried to do homework, but just couldn't focus. Sunny came out of his room once, and I chased him back in. I picked up a book I had been reading, but it didn't hold my attention. I went back to the TV, but there still wasn't anything interesting on. I put in an old video and turned it off a half hour later. Everything was boring.

I called Jenny and we talked for a few minutes. I warned her that Sunny had been sick and that I didn't know if whatever he had was contagious.

"Wonderful," she sighed. "That tops off the day perfectly."

"I know," I agreed.

"There was a message waiting for me from Jon when I got home," she said shyly.

"Really? What did it say?"

"That he was sorry and really wanted to talk to me. He apologized about six times on the machine."

"Good. He needed to."

"I know."

"Have you called him back?"

"Not yet."

I could hear Jenny's hesitation. "It was more Mike's fault than his," I said.

Jenny sighed. "I'm so glad you feel that way too. So you're dumping him, right?"

It was my turn to sigh. "Yeah, I guess I should."

"What do you mean, 'you guess'? He's been acting like a complete jerk!"

"Not all the time," I argued. "He can be really sweet."

"Think about it, Skye. Is he a sweet guy, or does he just act sweet when he's screwed up and he knows you're pissed at him?"

Suddenly I didn't want to talk about Mike. "You'd better go call Jon," I said. "And I better go too. I need to check on Sunny."

"Okay," she said. "I'll call you later."

"'Kay. Bye."

"Bye."

I hung up and wandered down the hall to my room. Even though I was mad at Mike, it still bothered me that Jenny thought he was a jerk. She wasn't around when he did the really sweet stuff. And I know I tend to whine about the bad stuff.

I still liked him, which confused me. He was so cute, and he could be really nice. And he was the first real boyfriend I'd ever had. I didn't want to lose him. I kept thinking about DeAnna and her stupid party. I was sure Mike would want to go now.

To get my mind off of Mike, I decided to see how Sunny was doing. I stopped at the linen closet between his room and mine and pulled out our old beat-up Monopoly game.

Sunny was sitting up in his bed, reading his book.

"How're you feeling?"

"A little better."

"Want to play Monopoly?"

His eyes lit up. "Yeah!"

"Want to play here or in front of the TV?"

"Let's go to the living room," he said, pushing his covers off.

As we walked down the hall, I asked him if he thought he could eat something.

He wrinkled his nose. "I'm kind of hungry, but I don't want to get sick again."

I set the box down on the table. "You set up the game and I'll go get us something to eat." I went to the kitchen and got out saltine crackers and two cans of soda. I sliced some cheese and put it on a separate plate for me. I put ice in two glasses and filled them with Sprite.

When I got back to the living room, Sunny had put *Star Wars*, his all-time favorite movie, in the VCR, and was almost done setting up the board.

"I'm banker," I said.

"You always get to be banker!"

"I'm banker, but I'll let you pick your piece first," I offered. When he continued to frown, I added, "And you can go first."

"Okay. I'm the hat."

I knew he had picked the hat because it was my favorite piece. "I'll be the dog," I said.

We had been playing for about forty minutes when the phone rang. Sunny jumped up. "Wait, Sunny. Just let the machine get it."

He looked at me. "Why?"

"Because I asked you to."

He sat back down. After the fourth ring, the answering machine clicked and we listened to Mom's voice cheerfully say that we were all too busy living life to answer the phone, so please leave a message and we'll call back when we're done living.

"Hi, Skye, it's Jenny. Just calling to see how everything's going. Give me a call."

I picked up the dice and rolled them. Sunny was watching me. I got an eight, which landed me on Pennsylvania Avenue. Neither of us owned it, but I was running low on cash and decided not to buy it. I pushed the dice across to Sunny.

"Why didn't you want to get the phone?" he asked.

I shrugged. "Just don't want to talk to anyone right now. I'll call Jenny after we finish the game."

He didn't look like he believed me, but he didn't ask any more questions. He just rolled the dice. I wasn't about to tell him I was screening the calls so I wouldn't have to talk to Mike, if he decided to call.

I was mad at Mike, but I liked having him for a boyfriend. I wanted him to apologize, but if he apologized, I was afraid I would take him back. It was easier just to avoid talking to him.

I won the first game of Monopoly. Then I fixed Sunny some chicken noodle soup before we started the second game. He said he was feeling fine.

While I was in the kitchen, I called Jenny. She wasn't home. Her mom said Jon had come by and picked her up about an hour ago. I asked her to have Jenny call me when she got home.

I tried to lose the second game, but Sunny wouldn't let me go bankrupt. Every time I couldn't pay the rent for landing on his properties, he gave me a loan. That game went on almost two hours before I finally convinced him to quit. I told him he was the winner because he had the most money.

After that, Sunny and I moved on to cards. I only got him to play a couple of games of gin rummy before he decided he wanted to play Go Fish. From there we moved on to Crazy 8s, and finally finished with a long game of War.

Finally, at ten o'clock, I told Sunny it was time for him to go to bed. I thought about calling Jenny, but decided I didn't need to get both of us in trouble for such a late call. I finished up the dishes and turned everything off.

Sunny was just coming out of the bathroom when I walked by him in the hall.

"Do you need any more Tylenol?" I asked him.

He shook his head. "I'm feeling much better," he said.

"Okay. Come get me if you need anything tonight. Sleep well."

I headed down the hall toward my room. Suddenly, from behind me, Sunny wrapped me in a big hug. "Thanks, Skye," he whispered. "I love you."

By the time I turned around, he was already disappearing into his room.

CHAPTER EIGHT

Sunday was long and slow. I spent the morning at Hannah's, listening to her talk about her date with Jeremy. He had taken her to a fancy restaurant, and then out dancing at a club. She had to be at work at one, so I went home.

Mom was happy to see me home early. She had been worried about Sunny Saturday night, but by Sunday afternoon, he was feeling better. She took us back to the mall and we saw *Somebody Save Scamp!*

At home, Mom grilled both Sunny and me on our classes and what we were doing at school. She asked Sunny about his swimming lessons, and, happily for me he didn't slip. He just told her how much fun he was having. I studied for a couple of hours, and then quizzed Sunny while Mom was out grocery shopping.

That evening, I jumped each time the phone rang. Once it was an old school friend of my mother's. She talked to him for a long time. The other time it was some telemarketer. Mike never called.

I resolved to ignore him at school. It turned out to be easier than I thought it would be, because he wasn't there on Monday.

I flirted shamelessly with Steve.

During American Lit, Jenny told me all about the romantic dinner Jon had made for her on Saturday night.

"At his house?" I asked.

"Uh-huh," she said.

"And his parents were gone?"

"Uh-huh," she said again.

"And all you did was eat dinner?"

"Uh-huh." She was blushing.

"Are you sure?"

She laughed. "Well, maybe that's not all we did. But we didn't do any-thing we haven't done before. I told him I was still mad about what hap-pened at the mall."

"What did he say?"

"He said that in the future he would be sure to ask me what I wanted to do, instead of trying to tell me what to do."

"Did he tell you what he and Mike did when they left?"

Jenny shook her head.

"Did he tell you what Mike said?"

Jenny gave an exasperated sigh. "I was talking to Jon about us, Skye. I didn't ask about you and Mike, because I thought that was over."

I decided to screen calls again Monday night so I wouldn't have to talk to Mike. It was easy. Nobody called.

I was miserable when I woke up Tuesday morning. Jenny was right, I realized. My brief relationship with Mike was over. I wasn't going to have the chance to dump him—apparently he had already dumped me.

I tried to tell myself that he wasn't worth it, but I kept thinking about the way I felt when I was alone with him. He made me feel attractive and desirable, and I had to admit it was a good feeling. I didn't want to give him up. Then I remembered his angry insistence on getting his way, and I got mad all over again. *If he doesn't want me anymore because I won't sleep with him*, I thought, *then fine, he can just go find someone else.*

I was also upset that I wouldn't have a chance to qualify for state today because Coach had decided to put everyone in off events.

Even being able to drive the car to school didn't get the scowl off my face. At least I didn't have to worry about being too early. I had overslept again. I pulled into the school parking lot just as the first bell was ring-ing. Sunny and I both ran into the building.

When I got to my locker the halls were almost empty. Since I was in a hurry, it only figured that I couldn't get my combination right till the third try. I opened my locker and stared in disbelief.

There, arranged in a vase on the shelf, were a half dozen short-stemmed red roses. An envelope with my name on it was leaning against the vase.

I tossed my bags into the locker, grabbed my binder, books, and the note, and took a quick smell of the roses before shutting the door and sprinting down the hall. I didn't make it to Government on time. Fortunately, it was my first tardy for that class.

I got my book out and handed in my homework. While we were reviewing our assignment, I managed to get the envelope open. I set the note inside my book to read it.

> Skye-
> I'm sorry I've been such a jerk lately. I wanted to call and apologize, but I got in a lot of trouble and I've been grounded from the phone. Then I was sick yesterday, so I didn't see you. Please forgive me. I promise to wait. You're worth it.
>
> Mike

I read through the note several times. I could feel my face flushing, and my stomach was all tingly. Part of me was still mad at Mike, but I couldn't stop smiling. At least he knew how to apologize.

A couple of times Steve smiled at me from across the room. I smiled back, but I really wasn't thinking about him. I couldn't get the last two sentences of Mike's note out of my mind.

I spent the rest of the day expecting Mike to come find me. He never did. I showed off the roses during lunch.

"Are you going to take him back?" Jenny asked.

I shrugged.

Jenny shook her head. "I'm not sure that's such a good idea, Skye."

"Why not?" I demanded. "You took Jon back."

"But that was different!"

"How? We were both at the same place at the same time and they tried to tell us what to do. And then they both left."

Jenny shook her head again. "I'm just saying that maybe you should think before you take Mike back. Remember what you were saying in the bathroom? About being scared of him sometimes? You shouldn't feel that way, Skye, and if you do, it's a sign that something is wrong."

I put my nose in the center of the roses and refused to look at her. Finally she sighed.

"Do what you want to do, Skye. Just make sure to dump him before he does anything to you that you don't want him to do."

"I will," I promised. A small part of me knew Jenny was right, that I shouldn't forgive him, but I wasn't ready to give up yet. Jenny and Jon had had longer to work things out. Mike and I could work things out too.

The rest of the day was fun. We watched movies in two classes, and we didn't have any homework. I got out of school ten minutes early to go to the meet. Sunny would have to walk over later by himself.

I took my roses with me. I knew that the hot, humid air inside the pool area wouldn't be good for them, but I wanted them with me anyway.

During warm-up I felt great. The water slid by me. Each stroke felt strong and easy. As we started our sprints, Coach called me over.

"How are you feeling today?"

"Great." I grinned.

He nodded. "You look really smooth." He hesitated for a moment, then said, "LaTonya is out sick today and can't swim. You want to give the 200 another crack?"

"Oh, yeah!"

"Okay, we'll pull you from the IM."

"Can I get the 500 too?" I asked.

He made a face at me. "Don't push your luck, Skye," he said. "Now get back in there and don't let me down."

I was wired. I hadn't been expecting to swim the 200, and now I had another chance. And I had roses in my bag. I felt fantastic. After the last sprints, I did a real lazy lap, so slow that I wasn't doing much more than floating down the pool and back.

At the shallow end, I ducked my head underwater, put my hands on the wall, and boosted myself out. Halfway out of the water, I noticed a pair of feet directly in front of me. I looked up. The feet belonged to Mike. He was holding a huge green towel with purple, pink, and blue fish on it.

"Hi," I said as I stood up. "Uh…aren't you supposed to be at practice?" I stammered.

"Hi," he said. "I skipped practice. I had something more important to do."

"Oh," I said. My mind was a blank. "So why are you here?"

"I'm here to see if I can make up for being a jerk."

I just looked at him.

"Did you get the note and flowers?" he asked.

I nodded.

He held the towel open in front of me. "I got you this too," he said, "But there wasn't room in your locker."

"Thanks," I said, reaching for it.

He shook his head and stepped forward, wrapping me in the towel and hugging me at the same time. "Can I have another chance?" he whispered into my ear.

I hugged him back. "I thought I already gave you one," I said, trying not to think about the rush I was feeling.

"I know," he said. "I'm stupid. I swear, this is the last second chance I'll need."

"It'd better be," I warned. I didn't sound as harsh as I wanted to when I added, "It's the only one you'll get."

Hannah swept by and managed to grab me as she did. "Sorry, Mike," she called over her shoulder, "Skye is needed at the team meeting."

"I'll be in the bleachers," he said. "Good luck."

I waved over my shoulder to him and followed Hannah into the locker room. She shook her head at me. "I thought you wanted to focus on going to state. Hugging someone as fine as Mike before your race is not a good idea."

"You're probably right."

"How about you give me all the gory details during diving?"

"Sounds good," I said.

I went over to a corner of the locker room and wedged myself into it. I was all wrapped up in the towel from Mike, and it felt like I was still in his arms. When I pulled the towel up to my face, I could smell his cologne. I forced myself to start taking deep breaths, and finally I began to relax.

Dimly, in the back of my mind, I could hear Coach talking. I stopped listening after he said my name for the 200 free. I put my head down on my knees and envisioned myself on the blocks. While Coach went through the rest of the lineup changes, I went through my race in my mind.

"Skye?"

I looked up into Christie's face.

"Come on, time to go do our cheer."

I shook my head. "I'll be out in a few minutes."

"Sure?"

"Yeah."

Usually I didn't miss the team cheer, no matter what. But I had just gotten myself focused on my race, and if I went out there to clown around and saw Mike in the bleachers, I would lose my concentration. So I stayed where I was. I could hear the cheers, both ours and the opposing team's. I heard the national anthem, and then I heard the start of the first relay. Mentally I went through my race one more time, and then I headed out to the deck.

I walked up to Coach to get my card.

"Where have you been?" he demanded. "I almost put Christie in for you."

"In the locker room," I said.

He looked at me skeptically, but there must have been something in my tone or the look on my face that stopped him from saying anything else. He simply handed me my card and wished me luck. That was all. No drilling on race plan or technique. He could tell I was ready.

I left my towel with the rest of my stuff on the deck and walked over to the starting blocks. Stretching out was part of my routine, and all the moves were light and easy. I had only been out of the water for ten minutes, so I was still loose and limber. I handed my card to the timer. I paced back and forth behind my lane three times.

I planted my feet and rolled my shoulders, letting my arms and hands dangle and jiggle limply at my side. With my chin on my chest, looking directly at the ground, breathing deeply, I was able to focus completely on the race at hand. The noise from the other swimmers and spectators was a dim background rumble.

The whistle blew. "Event number two, step up on the blocks."

Every word the announcer said was crisp and clear in my mind. I was finely tuned—seeing, hearing, feeling everything; yet seeing, hearing, feeling nothing but the upcoming race.

"Take your mark." The buzzer sounded. I exploded off the block, arching high. I felt the strength in my arms, legs, back. I could feel the energy all the way down to my toes as I pointed them, aiming for the perfect streamline. I hit the water, slicing down through it and then quickly popping back up to settle into my stroke.

At the end of the first length, I could tell I was starting at a faster pace than I had ever swum before. In the middle of my turn, I considered briefly holding back just a little, thinking I might kill myself with the fast pace and have nothing to finish with. As I took the first stroke off the turn, however, I knew I couldn't hold back. My mind and body were geared for this killer pace, and I would not drop back from it.

I blocked the other swimmers out of my mind. I didn't care where they were. If they were up in front or behind me, it didn't matter. I didn't see the crowd in the stands when I turned my head to breathe; all I saw was a blur. I was swimming my race, looking for a state qualifying time.

My legs began to burn when I was only halfway through the race. For a moment I faltered, afraid that I couldn't keep the pace. Then I tucked my head down and shifted my arms into overdrive. I would keep the pace. That was all there was to it.

The last fifty was pain. Pure, simple, uncomplicated pain. My legs were on fire, my lungs were ready to burst, my arms felt like lead being dragged through the water. Yet I don't think I could have stopped moving. That last lap felt like it took forever. For the first time, I allowed myself to look and see where my competition was. I couldn't see any of them. When I finished, I had no idea if I was in front of the field or behind it.

I touched the wall, and I couldn't even stand up. I leaned back instead, floating in the water, feeling every blood vessel in my body pounding, trying to get oxygen to my body. My ears were underwater so I could barely hear the cheers of the spectators. They seemed louder than usual. Sunny was screaming so loud I thought he might hurt himself. I stood up and looked at my coach and teammates.

Almost everyone was jumping up and down alongside the pool. I started to smile uncertainly. I looked at my timer. She had been waiting for me to look at her.

Her grin was huge. "2:04.67."

My jaw dropped. "Really?"

She nodded.

I jumped about three feet out of the water, throwing my arms in the air. *I did it! I qualified for state!* Suddenly, I wasn't tired. There was no pain. I was dancing through the water, shouting. I pulled myself up out of the pool and onto the deck, and immediately I was surrounded by friends and teammates, being hugged and congratulated on all sides. Coach actually left his position at the side of the pool and gave me a pat on the back while shaking my hand.

I turned and looked at the bleachers. Sunny was still jumping up and down, screaming his head off. Mike was yelling too, but when he saw me looking at him, he blew me a kiss. I had never felt so good. The whole world was in the palm of my hand.

CHAPTER NINE

Everything seemed to be falling into place. I called Mom as soon as I could, to tell her I made state. She was almost as excited as I was. She said she was really sorry she couldn't come home early that night to celebrate. When I woke up the next morning, a bouquet of four balloons was waiting for me in the living room, with a note from Mom, saying how proud she was.

Swimming, school, Mike: I had it all. Even dealing with Sunny was getting easier.

He really loved his swimming lessons. Sandra asked him to be an assistant in the evening classes and started having him work on more advanced skills. He was also proud because he had been moved up two levels in the Saturday lessons.

I should have known it was all too good to last.

One evening not long after I first qualified for state, Sunny and I were both doing homework.

"Skye?"

"What?" I didn't look up.

"I want to start swimming every day."

That got my attention. "You can't," I said, glancing over at him. I quickly went back to my Government book.

"Why not?"

"Because lessons are only on certain days, Sunny."

"So? I can practice on my own."

I laughed. "No, you can't."

"Why not? You do." He knew I sometimes practiced alone on Sunday mornings.

"Fine," I said. "When I go practice on Sunday, you can come swim too."

"But I want to practice every day."

I groaned. "Sunny, I really have to study for this test, okay?"

He had that stubborn look on his face. He put down his book and stood up, planting his feet in front of the sofa. "I *need* to practice every day. Sandra says I could get good."

"Sunny, I'm trying to tell you that you can only practice on the days of the lessons."

"They have open swim after your practice," he said.

"Yeah, right." I snorted. "Like I'm going to stay late at the pool every day just so you can practice. I don't think so." Shaking my head, I went back to my book, copying down definitions into my notebook. He was so quiet I thought he had left the room.

A minute later, though, I looked up and he was still standing there. "I'm sorry, Sunny. Four days a week will be enough for you. It's not like you're competing or anything."

"I *might* be."

I just barely choked back a laugh. "What do you mean?"

"Sandra says I could swim in the Special Olympics."

"Really?" I stared at him. I was impressed. After all, he had just started his swimming lessons a month ago. "When are they?"

He looked down at the carpet and shuffled his feet. "I don't know."

"You'll have to find out when they are. Then we can talk about it."

"But I need to practith more!" Sunny stomped his foot. "I'm not good enough yet!"

"I'm sorry, Sunny," I said again, trying to return to my book. "Four days a week. You're just going to have to accept it."

"I'll tell Mom," he said softly.

Startled, I turned back to him. "What?"

"I'll tell Mom," he repeated, louder this time.

I stared in disbelief. Usually I was the one who used this threat, even though it didn't really do any good. Sunny had never had anything on me to go telling Mom. Until now.

I shook my head. "No, you won't."

"Yes, I will."

"I told you, Sunny, I'll never trust you again if you tell. You're not going to tell. Besides, you promised."

"I want to practith every day."

"You can't!" I shouted. I had to shout. I was sick of going in circles about it.

"Yeth, I can!" he yelled back. "You have to wait for me after your practith. Then I won't tell."

I couldn't believe it. He had me trapped. I couldn't believe it!

∽

At first I hated staying late every day, but after a while, I actually began to enjoy it. I hung around with the lifeguards, joking around and chatting about things. Listening to them and watching them work, I learned a lot about being a guard. Gail and I talked about the upcoming lifeguard training class and tried to figure out the best days and times for it. The fact that she really wanted me in the class made me feel important.

Life settled into a comfortable routine. One thing seemed strange, though. Once I qualified for state, I was able to qualify at every meet. At the most recent meet, not only did I requalify in the 200 free, but in the 500 as well. And by now I knew I had secured a starting spot on the 400 free relay. Coach said I had overcome a mental block.

I was also breezing through all of my classes. I had never had straight A's before, but now it was like A's were falling into my lap.

The only possible snag I could think of was homecoming. It had been postponed this year because they had had to refinish the gym floor after a pipe burst. For a while, I had been afraid that the dance would end up being the night of our conference championship meet, or maybe even state. Luckily, the dance was rescheduled for the week before conference, two weeks before state.

I didn't want to miss homecoming for two reasons: one, I was incredibly excited about going with Mike, and two, I was nominated for junior class princess.

Then I found out Jenny was nominated for the royal court too, and so were Mike and Jon! The day they announced the nominations, Jenny and I went out to lunch with Mike and Jon to celebrate, joking about being half of the homecoming royalty.

I was stunned and a little nervous about the nomination. It would be hard if either Jenny or I won, because then the other would have lost. And if Mike or Jon were chosen and Jenny and I weren't, they would have to escort other girls at the game and then again at the dance. DeAnna was one of the senior girls who had been nominated for queen. The thought of seeing Mike escorting her anywhere made me ill.

I think Mike could tell I was anxious. He was very sweet to me. The weekend after I qualified for state, he took me out for a fancy dinner. And he was such a gentleman, he hardly even tried to kiss me. In fact, I think I kissed him more than he kissed me.

He started walking me to at least two classes every day, and skipped his fifth hour class twice to go out to lunch with me. We kept getting together while Sunny had his swimming lessons, and he didn't try to get me to stay home with him. He always took me out instead. I was in heaven.

Then, at the worst possible time, all hell broke loose.

First off, Mom told me I couldn't buy the dress I had picked out at the mall for homecoming. Even though deep down I had known we wouldn't be able to afford it, I still got really upset when she said no.

"I have to have a decent dress," I wailed. "I'll pay you back somehow."

"I'd love for you to have an expensive new dress for the dance, Skye, but we simply don't have the money right now."

"Well, fine, then. I might as well not go to homecoming at all!" I retorted.

Mom raised an eyebrow at me. "If you're going to take that attitude, no, you shouldn't go."

Quickly I changed my tone. "Mom," I pleaded. "You don't understand. This is a really big deal. Everyone's going to be looking at me if I'm elected princess. I've got to have that dress!"

Mom cocked her head at me. "When did you get such a big ego?" she asked. "If you're not careful, Skye, someone's going to mistake your head for a hot air balloon."

"Mother," I said, trying to sound calm. "I'm not being conceited. This is my first time ever to be nominated for homecoming princess. If I'm elected, I'll be presented to the whole school. That's why everyone's going to be looking at me."

"Believe me, Skye, a lot fewer people care about the homecoming queens and princesses than you realize," Mom said dryly.

"Please, Mom, isn't there any way I can get the dress?"

"Of course there is, honey," she said warmly, but with a dangerous glint in her eye. "You can use your own money."

"You know I don't have enough money!"

"It's not my fault you spend money so quickly. I've been paying for the swimming lessons, and that's put a tough stretch on my budget. In fact," she said, "I just barely had enough to pay you for last week."

I could only hope my face didn't look as guilty as I felt. Last week I had made the final payment for Sunny's lessons.

"And I know there are times you use your lunch money for something other than lunch," she continued. "If you had saved that money, maybe you could afford a dress. But I can't buy that one for you. I'm sorry. Couldn't you find a cheaper one at the discount store or borrow one from Jenny?"

I stared into space for a few moments. Then I sighed. It was a lost cause. "Okay. I'll call Jenny."

As usual my best friend came through for me. Her cousin Alison, who is about my size, said she'd be glad to loan me the dress she had worn to her school's Valentine dance last year. It actually looked great on me.

The next thing to go wrong was that Sunny got sick. It wasn't a serious cold or anything, but the problem is that every cold Sunny gets completely knocks him out, both physically and emotionally.

As a precaution, Mom told him he couldn't go swimming for at least a week, and he pitched an absolute fit. He cried and screamed for so long that he actually turned blue. He kept on until he threw up. That finally quieted him down a little.

Then he tried to blackmail me into letting him swim in spite of Mom's orders. He threatened again to tell Mom about the lessons. But I didn't intend to give in this time. First I told him she wouldn't believe him; she'd just think he was hallucinating from the fever. When that didn't work, I stooped really low. Sunny is terrified of hospitals. He's had to go to the hospital a lot because he gets sick so often. I told him I'd tell Mom he'd had a relapse and needed to go to the hospital. I felt bad, but I was glad my threat worked and he quit talking about telling on me.

While Sunny was sick, I didn't get to see Mike very much. Mike was pretty understanding until the week before homecoming, but then he started getting upset about it.

He met me at my locker Thursday morning. "Skye, this is getting ridiculous. I haven't seen you all week."

"You've seen me at school."

He rolled his eyes. "Like that counts for anything. I want, no, I *need* some time alone with you. Skip practice today."

"No way. I've got to practice."

"You've already qualified several times. You deserve a break."

"Just because I've qualified doesn't mean I'll do well at state. I doubt I'll even make the top twelve."

"So why not take a day off? You've made it to state, but you're not going to place, so it really doesn't matter."

"It does matter, Mike," I groaned. "This is serious to me."

"That's the problem," he argued. "You take everything too seriously. You need to lighten up and have some fun."

I glared at him. "I have a lot of fun. Maybe you need to be serious more often."

"No," he said, shaking his head. "Life will get serious later. I don't need to be serious now."

"Well, I'm not skipping practice and I have to stay home with Sunny this weekend. I'm sorry, but I can't get out of it." Mike's eyes clouded over and I hurried on. "But Mom promised to come home early next Saturday night. She can't wait to meet you. And I can't wait to spend the whole night dancing with you."

He laughed a little. "I still can't believe your mom actually thought you could find a date for Sunny so he could go, too."

I felt a little defensive. "She just wants what's best for him. Besides, who's to say that he won't get a date to the dance all by himself?"

Now Mike really laughed. "Right, like that'll ever happen."

"You never know. He's a sweet kid."

"He's a retard," Mike said flatly.

I stared at him. "I can't believe you just said that!" As I slammed my locker, I just missed his fingers and made him jump. "You know, you can be a real jerk sometimes."

I turned around and walked away. I was furious. I hated that word. Sunny has Down syndrome, and he needs a little extra time to do things, but he's not a retard. He's just a person who needs help sometimes. I know Sunny annoys me, but he's part of my family. He's my brother. I'm supposed to complain about him. I can insult him because I know him; no one else has that right. And besides, half the time he really isn't as bad as I say he is anyway.

I think it took Mike the better part of the day to figure out that I was avoiding him because he had really made me angry.

Mike called me that night. "I'm sorry," was the first thing he said.

"You should be."

"I didn't mean it. I'm just frustrated. I was getting spoiled seeing you so much, and now I'm selfish. I want that time with you."

"I know, Mike, and I want that time, too. But it doesn't mean you can call Sunny a retard."

"I know, I know," he sighed, and I could just picture him running his hand through his hair.

"Hey," I said, changing the subject, "Mom's going to be home on Sunday, and since I've been taking care of Sunny at night all week, she said I could have the whole day to myself."

"She's not going to make it family day again?"

"No. She knows I need a break."

"Can I have you to myself all day?"

I laughed. "Jenny and I need to go to the mall when it opens in the morning, but we'll be back by one, so I could come over around two."

"And then I get you for the rest of the afternoon?"

"Yeah."

"Okay," he said. "I can handle that." I could tell he was grinning.

Even though it was already Thursday night, I felt like Sunday would never come. But somehow I managed to make it through the rest of the week.

On Sunday Jenny's mother took us to the mall. I couldn't get our car because Mom was planning to take Sunny to the park if it didn't rain. I was looking forward to wandering the mall, but at the same time, I was hoping Jenny would finish her shopping within an hour so we could get home early and I could go to Mike's. But Jenny is a die-hard shopper, and she was upset that we only had two hours.

Of course, not only was Jenny picking up her dress, but she also wanted to get shoes and some new makeup, and she confessed that she thought it would be cool to have a little matching purse for the dance as well. There were times I almost hated Jenny, and this was one of those times. It seemed so unfair that she could just go shopping whenever she wanted and buy almost anything. Her parents gave her a large weekly allowance plus lunch money. Her mother had given her a hundred dollars for extras for the dance. Life just wasn't fair.

Because I was feeling a little envious, I was kind of quiet for a while. Jenny knows I have a hard time shopping with her. But she's so bubbly and gets so excited about the silliest things, that soon I was laughing and joking with her. We had a great time.

She tried on the red satin dress that she had left to be altered. It fit her beautifully and suited her dark hair and complexion perfectly. She found a little black purse, and decided to get black hose and shoes to go with the outfit. She was going to be gorgeous, and I told her so.

I couldn't believe we stayed the whole time. In fact, we stayed so long, we were late meeting her mom, and she chewed us out on the way home. Of course, we were both giggling so much, we really didn't care. Her mom didn't mean it anyway, and we knew it.

Mike didn't live far from Jenny, so I walked to his house from hers. It probably would have made more sense to call him and have him come pick me up, but I was so excited that I just wanted to get over there. Besides, this way I could surprise him.

It worked, too. He opened the door and stared at me for a few seconds before a huge grin took over his face. Seeing that smile made me feel great.

"Hey, handsome," I said, reaching up for a hug.

"Hello, beautiful," he replied, hugging me hard against him.

I lifted my face and was rewarded with a long, passionate, open-mouthed kiss. After a minute I pulled back to look at him.

"Mmmm," I said, melting into his hug. I took a deep breath, absorbing his cologne.

"Is Sunny better?" Mike asked into my hair.

"Yeah," I said.

"Good, 'cause I don't want to go through another week like that."

I laughed. "Did you miss me?"

"More than you know," he said, stepping back into the entryway. I followed him down the hall to his room. He shut the door after I got in.

Wary, I looked at him. "Are your parents home?" I asked.

"Nope," he said, and his grin got even bigger. He crossed the room to his bed and sat down.

I just stood there looking at him.

He patted the mattress next to him. "Come on, Skye, come sit down."

I was nervous, but I walked over and sat down next to him. He turned me so I was facing him and began to cover me with kisses—my face, my neck, my shoulders. I was tingling all over.

I'm not quite sure how it happened, but the next thing I knew, we were lying down on the bed on our sides, facing each other. I started to say no, but he covered my mouth with his, and I lost myself in the kiss.

His hands had been straying everywhere, but suddenly I was aware that they were now straying over bare skin. He had unhooked my bra. I gasped when his hand passed over my breast. I wrenched my head away.

"Mike!" I wasn't ready for this. Yes, it was fun at first, and yes, it felt incredibly good to have him touch me. But I sensed that I was losing control of the situation.

He rolled over on top of me, kissing me again.

I was trying to stop his hands, stop his mouth, but I couldn't do either. I was beginning to get angry, and a little scared. He was being too aggressive. We were both breathing heavily. I tried to shift out from under him, but he was too heavy. Finally I was able to turn my head away from him.

"Mike, stop it!"

He tried to kiss me again.

"Mike!"

"Skye," he breathed, still trying to kiss me. I put my hands on his shoulders and tried to shove him away. I felt his hand at my waist, and in the next moment, the zipper on my jeans was undone.

"Stop it! Mike, stop!" I was trying to squirm out from under him.

His hands no longer felt warm, strong, and friendly. They were now demanding, insistent, invading. I was unable to catch my breath. It felt like I was drowning on dry land. "Mike!"

"You're ready, Skye," he said, biting my neck. "You know you want to." His hands were everywhere.

I couldn't stop his hands or his mouth. I tried again to get out from underneath him. I didn't make it, but I did get one leg in between his. I couldn't breathe. I felt sick. His hand was going down my pants. I was in a panic.

I tried one more time. "Mike, *stop!*"

He didn't, so I brought my knee up as fast and hard as I could.

That got his attention. He had seemed heavy before, when he was moving, but that was nothing compared to his dead weight as he groaned and collapsed on top of me. He wasn't trying to hold me down any more, so I gave him a shove and struggled out from under him.

I sat up and almost fell off the bed. I zipped my pants and refastened my bra and pulled my shirt down as I stumbled toward the door. He was cursing into the mattress. I ran down the hall and out of the house, afraid that at any moment I'd hear him behind me. I kept running, even when I got to the corner. The brisk wind kept drying the tears off my face.

CHAPTER TEN

I was halfway to my house before I realized that I couldn't go home. If I went home this upset, Mom would have a lot of questions for me. Questions I didn't want to answer. I didn't want to go to Jenny's either. I didn't know where to go. I just kept walking.

The steady wind blew in heavy black rain clouds, threatening a thunderstorm. I didn't care if it rained. I hoped it would rain, a hard, cold downpour.

I was shaking all over. Now that I was out of Mike's house, feelings were crashing down on me at once. I was hurt, angry, scared, confused, embarrassed, and I couldn't stop shaking. I was afraid I was going to throw up. I had to keep moving. My feet just went. I was too focused on my churning insides to notice anything around me.

The shaking gradually stopped, but my mind was stuck in front of a TV, watching a videotape that was on a loop. I kept seeing Mike, kept feeling his hands on me, kept feeling the shock and disbelief and anger. I felt like I was strangling on my fear, even though I was outside and away from his touch. I kept hearing his groan. Maybe I had really hurt him.

I couldn't stop the tape. It played over and over again. I didn't want to think about it, but I couldn't turn it off.

When I finally stopped and looked around, I realized I was less than a block from the pool. Seeing where I was made it seem like a weight was lifted off my shoulders. I had, in a way, gone home. This was where I belonged. This was where I was safe. I knew the people here, I knew what I would find, and I knew I could go inside and not be questioned.

Opening the doors to the lobby, I was immediately embraced by the warm, humid, chlorinated air. It smelled and felt wonderful. I could hear the strangely muffled, yet still echoing shouts of the kids who were in the pool area, playing. Gail was behind the desk. Everything was exactly the way it should be.

It was a relief to step into the lobby, but I was still shaking inside. Gail looked up at me.

"Hey there!" She grinned. "It's a family day, huh?"

"What do you mean?"

"Your mom and brother just went in."

There was a sinking feeling in the pit of my stomach. "Tell me you're kidding."

Gail gave me a strange look. "Why would I kid about something like that?"

I leaned over on the desk, groaning. *Could my day possibly get any worse?* "Gail," I mumbled, "please tell me you didn't say anything about the swimming lessons."

She frowned and cocked her head to one side. "Well, no," she began, "not really."

I groaned again. "What did you say?"

"Just that Sunny had been working hard and practicing a lot."

"Really? That's all you said?"

"Yeah."

"You're sure?"

"Yes."

"Positive?"

"Yes. Skye, what's going on?" Gail looked a little annoyed.

"Nothing, nothing."

She shook her head. "I don't think so," she said. "You look awful. Are you feeling all right?"

"Look, I've got to go," I said. I was near tears again. I couldn't handle this right now. "Please don't tell my mom or Sunny I was here."

"Skye—"

I ignored her as I turned around and practically ran back out the door. The cold wind was still blustering, whipping at my hair and jacket. I headed toward our house. No one would be there. I could curl up and maybe the world around me would disappear. I kept my head down.

"Skye!"

I nearly jumped out of my skin. I looked up and was amazed to see Jenny and her mom pulling up alongside me. Jenny reached back and unlocked the door.

I climbed in gratefully. "What're you doing?" we both asked each other at the same time.

Her mom laughed. "I swear, it's amazing how similar the two of you are."

"Really, Skye, what are you doing?" Jenny turned around in the seat to look at me. "I thought you were going over to Mike's."

With a pointed glance at her mom, I shook my head. "No, it didn't work out." I could see the confusion on Jenny's face. She could tell something was wrong. I didn't want her asking anything else, so I quickly added, "What're you doing?"

Her face lit up. "Shopping."

"Again?"

"That's what *I* said," Jenny's mom remarked.

Jenny laughed. "I just needed to get a couple more things," she said. "So, since I don't get my driver's license until next month, I got my wonderful, beautiful, kind, understanding mother to take me."

Through the rearview mirror I saw Jenny's mom roll her eyes. "You're not going to get anything else, Jenny. You can quit kissing up."

We all laughed. I was thankful to have my mind on something else, even for a moment.

"Should I take you home?" Jenny's mom asked.

"Or do you want to come over to my house?" Jenny added.

"I'll come over, if it's okay." The words came out of my mouth before I had time to think.

"Of course it's okay," Jenny assured me. "Isn't it, Mom?"

Her mom laughed again. "You know it's okay," she said. "Sometimes it seems like I have two daughters."

Minutes later we were at Jenny's house, and Jenny whisked me up to her room. She shut the door behind us, and then turned to me.

"Okay, spill it," she commanded.

I started to say "Spill what?" in my best innocent voice, but before I could open my mouth, the tears were streaming down my face again.

"Skye?" Jenny asked, alarmed.

I couldn't move. I think I was making a strange squeaking noise instead of actually breathing. The tears wouldn't stop.

Jenny gave me a hug and kept saying, "It's okay, Skye, it's okay." She steered me over to her bed and we both sat down.

Slowly, I calmed down and was able to tell her what had happened. She stayed next to me, patting me on the back, making encouraging sounds like "uh-huh" and "okay," but not really saying anything.

When she was sure I was done talking, she muttered, "I knew Mike could be a jerk, but I had no idea...." She shook her head briskly. "So what are we going to do about it?"

"We?" I asked. "We're not going to do anything about it."

"Something has to be done," Jenny said, "And I'm not going to make you do it alone."

"There's nothing to do," I said.

"What do you mean by that?"

I shook my head. "I mean there's nothing to do. I'm not going to see him any more. That's all."

"That's all? That can't be all!"

I looked at her. The tears were threatening again. "There's nothing else to do."

"Nothing else? How about reporting him?"

"To who, Jenny? For what?" I asked. "He didn't do anything."

"Wrong," Jenny said flatly. "What he *did* was not stop. And that's something."

"Okay, so he didn't stop when I asked him to. But he didn't rape me either. I got him to stop. There's nothing to report." I paused. "It'd just be my word against his, anyway. He didn't force me to come to his house or go in his bedroom." I flopped back on the bed and put my hands over my face. "Oh, God, Jenny. He could say anything. Why didn't I...."

Jenny got up and opened her door.

"Where are you going?" I asked quickly.

"I'm going to ask my mom what we should do."

I bolted for the door and shut it hard. "No way." I leaned against the door, both for support and to keep her from leaving the room.

"Skye," Jenny began.

"No!" I almost shouted. "Jenny, just let it go, okay?" I begged. "Please?"

"Let me just go ask her," Jenny said again.

"No!" I repeated. "He didn't really hurt me."

Jenny was shaking her head. "It may not have been rape, but I still think it was sexual assault or something. I want to go ask my mom."

I was crying again. "*Please* don't, Jenny."

She looked at me, and I could see the confusion and hurt I was feeling reflected on her face.

"I don't want to make a big deal about this." I was beginning to sob again, and I was barely able to finish. "I don't want people to know. God, I don't want anyone to know!"

Jenny held me again while I cried. This time it didn't take me quite as long to settle down.

"Please promise me you won't tell anyone, not your mom, not even Jon."

"Skye," Jenny said.

"Promise!" I insisted.

She sighed. "Do you promise to tell someone the instant you're ready to talk?"

"I promise," I said instantly.

She didn't say anything.

"Jenny," I prodded.

"I promise not to tell anyone," she said reluctantly.

We turned back from the door, and Jenny sat down on her bed again. I took the chair by her desk.

"We've got to do something."

"Jenny," I groaned. I was beginning to wish I had never told her.

"I don't mean we have to tell an adult," Jenny said. "But we can't just let him get away with this."

"He didn't get away with it," I said. "He wasn't moving very well when I left him."

Jenny began to giggle. "At least you got his immediate attention."

"To say the least," I said.

"Did you do it really hard?" Jenny asked.

"Oh, yeah, as hard as I could."

"Maybe he won't be able to play football. You know, maybe he'll have a groin injury or something."

I laughed weakly. "You're really enjoying this, aren't you?"

Jenny gave me a mischievous grin. "If you won't let someone else take care of it, then you and I will. I'm sure we can come up with something terrible to do to him."

We spent the next half hour concocting schemes on how to get back at Mike. I knew we weren't going to do any of them, but it still made me feel a little better, and Jenny really enjoyed it. In the middle of all our plotting, though, she suddenly sat up straight. "Oh no!" she shrieked.

"What?" I turned around, trying to see what had freaked her out so much.

"Homecoming!"

I looked at her blankly for at least three seconds before I realized what she was thinking. "I don't have a date," I said, in shock. I had been nominated for princess and I didn't have a date. "I'm not going to homecoming," I said, as if trying to prove it to myself.

"Of course you're going to homecoming!" Jenny exclaimed. "You have to be there."

"Not without a date. I won't go."

"Well, then we've got to get you another date, Skye."

I stared at her. "Jenny, homecoming is Saturday. There's no way I'll find a date now!"

"There is a way," Jenny insisted. "And we're going to find it."

"How?" I asked her.

We tried to think of someone I could ask. Everyone we came up with was already going with somebody else. After a few minutes, Jenny jumped up, grinning.

"Of course!" she said. "Why didn't I think of him before?" She went to her bookshelf, pulled out the school directory, and picked up the phone while she flipped through the pages.

"Jenny? Jenny, what are you doing?" I watched in alarm as she began dialing. "Who are you calling?" I tried to hang up the phone on her, but she pulled it out of my reach.

"You'll see," she said smugly, putting the phone to her ear.

"If it's a date for me, I think I should have some say about it."

Jenny shook her head. "No, Skye, you—Hello, is Steve there?" she said into the phone.

I felt my cheeks get warm. Jenny had the phone, and there was absolutely nothing I could do. She was in control. I certainly didn't want him to know I was there, so I couldn't say anything.

"Hi, Steve, this is Jenny, from trig class.... Yeah, how are you doing?... Oh, I'm doing all right, I guess.... I don't want to go back to school tomorrow.... Well, listen, the reason I'm calling..."

I felt myself tensing up all over. Jenny wasn't even looking at me.

"...is because I couldn't remember if we had any homework.... Uh-huh.... Okay, page 215.... Uh-huh...."

She actually pretended to write on an imaginary pad of paper!

"Was that one through twenty-five odd?... Okay, great. I really appreciate it.... How was your weekend?... Really? That sounds cool.... Yeah. Are you ready for homecoming week?... Don't forget tomorrow's hat day.... By the way, who are you taking to the dance?"

I knew I had made a mistake in staying in the room. I should have left, so I wouldn't hear everything like this.

"Oh really?... Bummer.... Are you sure you can't get out of it?... Yeah, that does suck.... Well, listen, I've got to get going. Thanks for the assignment info.... See you tomorrow.... Bye."

Jenny hung up the phone and finally turned to face me.

"He can't go," I said.

"He's got to work."

I shook my head in admiration. "You did that very well."

"What do you mean?"

"You were sly," I said. "It sounded like a totally normal conversation. He didn't even suspect what you were up to!"

"Well, of course," Jenny said, tossing her head. "What did you expect from the master of finesse?"

I sighed. "Well, it was a good try. Thanks."

"We'll think of someone, Skye. Just because we didn't get first choice doesn't mean you're staying home Saturday night."

I had to laugh. "Thanks, Jenny. It's really sweet of you to try to help me out like this."

"I'm not doing this only for you, Skye."

"You're not?"

"I'm doing it for me. The dance would be way too dull without my best friend there."

That called for another hug.

When I said good-bye for the evening, I made her promise again not to tell anyone about what had happened with Mike.

"And I do mean anyone, Jen, not even Jon."

She pretended to pout. "But if I don't tell Jon, how am I supposed to convince him to beat the tar out of Mike?"

I smiled. "They're good friends," I reminded her. The panicky feeling hit me again. "You don't think Mike would tell Jon, do you?"

"No. Somehow I doubt he'll want anyone to know about your method of rejection."

"I hope you're right. Please, Jen, I'm counting on you to keep this to yourself."

"I promise. I won't say a word. I won't say I like keeping quiet, but I'll do it for you."

"Thanks. I'll see you at school tomorrow."

I walked home in the gray afternoon. Talking with Jenny had calmed me down a lot, but my stomach was still all fluttery. I dreaded going home. I was trying to think of what I'd tell Mom.

I came up with all sorts of excuses, but I didn't like any of them. Finally I decided that the best thing to do was not say anything at all. I was afraid that if I even tried to talk about Mike, I'd start crying again.

I was curled up in front of the TV by the time Sunny and Mom came home. I almost went to my room to avoid being with them, but I simply didn't have the energy. I was physically and emotionally exhausted. They were going to want to talk, but I wasn't sure I could follow a normal conversation. I didn't feel normal anymore.

Their hair was still wet, and they were both laughing. For a minute, I almost felt jealous.

"I'm going to go get changed, Mom," Sunny said, going down the hall.

"Skye," Mom said, flopping down on the couch next to me, "you've done a great job with Sunny. He's doing really well."

"Thanks," I said. Now instead of feeling envious, I felt guilty.

"He did say something that confused me, though," Mom said.

"Oh? What?" I was terrified that Sunny had slipped and I had been found out.

"He said something about being moved up. What does that mean?"

"Oh." I forced myself to laugh. "That. I just told him that he was doing really well. Then I told him that I was moving him up out of the beginner level. You know, kind of like he was taking lessons."

Mom grinned. "Well, he was sure excited about it."

We were both quiet for a few minutes. I was sweating all over. I just hoped I wouldn't start shaking again.

"Want to go out to dinner and celebrate?" Mom asked.

"Celebrate?" I looked at her, trying to focus on what she was saying. It was like the world around me was going on normally, but I was stuck in some twilight zone. I was beginning to wonder if I would ever feel normal again.

"Skye?" Mom looked at me funny. "Are you still with us?"

"Um, yeah," I said. "Can we afford to go out?"

"Sure," Mom said easily.

I stared at her and after a few moments she finally said in an exasperated tone, "Well, aren't you going to ask *how* we can afford it?"

"How can we afford it?"

"I got a raise!"

"When?" I asked.

"Friday," she said, beaming.

"And you waited till now to tell us?"

"I wanted to surprise you both with a nice dinner, but it turns out I can't keep a secret very well. I had to tell Sunny about it today at the pool."

"A 'nice' dinner?" I asked suspiciously.

She shrugged. "I've got two-for-one coupons for Arturo's," she said. "Is that nice enough for you?"

"Oh, yeah!" I said, trying to sound enthusiastic. The last thing I wanted to do was go out to dinner.

"I'm sorry I didn't get this raise a little earlier, Skye."

"Why?"

"Because then you might have been able to buy the homecoming dress you wanted. Not that you won't knock 'em dead anyway," she added, kissing me on the forehead. "I'll just get changed and then we can go."

She was talking about homecoming and dinner. Life was going on. How was I going to make it when I couldn't even think anymore?

Sunny came back into the living room just a few minutes after she left.

"Did you have fun?" I asked.

He nodded. "She doesn't swim very well."

I managed a laugh. "I know. I've seen her swim." Then I looked at him. "Thanks for not telling Mom about the lessons."

He just nodded.

"Did you talk to her about Special Olympics?"

He shook his head.

"Why not?" I asked.

He shrugged. "I'm not sure I want to go."

I stared at him. "What do you mean? It's all you've been talking about lately."

"It's no big deal," he said, looking up at me through his shaggy bangs.

I was trying to figure out what he meant by that when Mom came back into the living room.

On the way to the restaurant, I sat in the back and barely heard Mom and Sunny chattering in the front seat. I stared out the window and saw absolutely nothing. When we got to Arturo's, we were seated almost immediately. After the waiter took our order, Mom leaned forward and looked at me.

"Are you okay? You're awfully quiet."

"I'm just tired," I said.

"You sure that's all?" She tried to put her hand on my forehead.

I grimaced and pulled away. "I'm fine, Mother."

Mom looked sideways at Sunny. "Should I tell her my other surprise? Think it would wake her up?"

Sunny nodded. "Tell her," he said.

Mom was practically bouncing in her chair. I couldn't remember ever seeing her so excited.

"Guess what?"

"What?"

"You're supposed to guess!" Sunny complained.

I groaned. "Mom, I have absolutely no idea. Just tell me."

"It's something you've wanted for a long time."

"I don't know.... A pony."

"Come on, Skye, guess!"

"I just did."

"You're not being any fun," Mom said. She wasn't bouncing in her chair anymore.

"I told you, I'm tired."

She sighed. "Fine. Spoil my big surprise."

"I'm sorry," I began.

"Just because I actually managed to pull getting November sixth off...." Mom let her voice trail off and just grinned at me.

I couldn't believe it, so I didn't say anything.

"Don't tell me I got the wrong day, Skye," she said in a panicky voice. "State is the sixth, right?"

"You really got it off?"

"Yeah!" She was bouncing again. "I'll get to see my baby swim. It's been ages since I've seen you swim in a meet, but now I get to see you at state!"

As the news sank in, I started to smile. "Oh, Mom, that's so cool! I can't believe you got it off!" I grinned. Just a few moments ago, I hadn't thought it would ever be possible for me to smile again, but here I was grinning. Mom would be at state.

I looked over at Sunny. He was folding and unfolding his napkin. His face was pale. "Sunny? Is something wrong?" I asked.

Mom looked at him. Now she put her hand on his forehead. "You feeling okay, honey?"

He pulled away from her. "I'm fine."

It dawned on me that Sunny might be feeling a little jealous with all the attention focused on me, so I asked him if he had found out about Special Olympics.

"Special Olympics?" Mom asked, looking up from her salad.

"Some of the guards have watched him swim and think he'd be good enough for the Special Olympics," I explained. "That's why he's practicing every chance he gets. Now we just have to find out when it is and get an entry form."

Mom's face brightened again. "Sunny, that's wonderful," Mom said, putting her arm around him and giving him a squeeze. "Why didn't you tell me before?"

He just shrugged. "It's no big deal," he said.

"Well, let's find out when they are. Who knows, maybe I'll be able to see you swim, too!"

He just shrugged again. After a few seconds, though, he lifted his fork and began picking at his salad. By the time our main courses came, Mom had him explaining the experiments his science teacher had done in class yesterday. I tried to follow their conversation and ask a question from time to time, so I would look normal. Mom asked me about Mike once, and I gave a short, nothing kind of answer, and the topic was dropped.

CHAPTER ELEVEN

Monday was pure torture. I felt ill all morning, convinced every time I turned around that I would see Mike. I avoided all the places where we usually met. I even took a different hallway on my way to lunch.

"Bad news," Jenny said, sitting down across from me at the table.

"What?" I asked tiredly.

"Mike's been telling everyone that he dumped you."

I looked at her. "Excuse me?"

"Hang on, Skye, it gets worse. He's also saying you were calling him constantly, that you always had to be with him, and you were just basically suffocating him. And…"

"And what?"

"He told Jon he ended it because you weren't any good in bed."

"Oh, God." I put my head in my hands. "I can't believe him." I looked up at her. "Please tell me that's all."

Jenny frowned.

"Oh, no." I put my head back into my hands. "You might as well tell me everything."

"He's already got a date for homecoming," Jenny said.

"No."

"Yes."

"DeAnna Garcia?"

She nodded.

I closed my eyes and took a deep breath.

"So what are we going to do?" Jenny asked.

"What do you mean?"

"I mean, we can't let him spread lies about you like this."

"Well, we can't tell people the truth," I said.

"Why not?"

"Jenny, you promised!"

"Okay, okay."

After a few minutes, when I hadn't said anything, Jenny asked if I had called anyone last night.

"For what?"

"Skye!" I could tell she was exasperated. "We've got to get you a date for homecoming!"

"Jenny, you know, I just don't care anymore. Okay?"

She slammed her palm down on the table, making me jump and look up at her. "Don't you dare!" she hissed at me. "If you're not going to make him admit to what he did, don't you dare roll over and just let him walk on you! Show some pride. Show a little backbone. Don't you dare let him beat you!"

I was startled. She was really angry. "Jenny—" I began.

"No, Skye, you can't let him get off this easy. You are going to go to homecoming with a date, you are going to hold your head high, and you are going to show him that he does not matter at all!" She finished in a harsh whisper. "And you are going to make him pay for trying to rape you!" She pushed her chair back from the table and walked away before I could say anything.

I stared after her for a few minutes. She was right. I opened my notebook to a blank page and wrote down the names of a couple of guys I knew at other schools. All I could see was Mike's face. I felt him shifting his weight on top of me, I felt his lips on my neck, his hands on my skin. Then I thought about what he had told Jon. I wanted to kill Mike. I wanted to die. I wanted Mike to choke on his mouth guard during the homecoming game. I wanted to go away somewhere far away and never come back.

I tore out the sheet of paper and threw it in the trash on my way out of the cafeteria.

I didn't see Jenny again until art class. I apologized at the same time she did, and we both laughed. Then I told her she was right, and that I would go to the dance. During class, she and I were able to come up with a pitifully small list of names. Then we picked the best order for calling them. It looked like I would be spending most of the night on the phone. I just hoped I'd be able to maintain normal conversations.

Steve caused a small panic when he came up behind us and asked us what we were doing. I was pretty sure we had enough of the paper covered that he didn't see the list. We talked to him for a few minutes before our teacher chased him back to his table. As he walked away, Jenny gave me a sympathetic look. I could almost hear her saying, "Too bad we couldn't get him!"

I managed to make it through the rest of the afternoon in a kind of daze. Deb came up in the hall and tapped me on the shoulder during a passing period, and I screamed. In two of my classes, the teachers asked for homework that I had completely forgotten about. Luckily, none of my teachers called on me in class.

When I went to meet Hannah at her locker after school, she wasn't there yet. Rumor had it that she and Lou were getting back together again—no big surprise. I assumed she was going to be a little late because of him, so I just headed over to the pool by myself.

When I walked in the door, Gail was behind the desk.

"Hey, Gail," I said.

"Hey." She looked at me. "You okay?"

I shrugged. "Yeah. Sorry I was kind of rude yesterday."

"What happened?"

Shaking my head, I said, "I'd rather not talk about it. I'll see you later." I turned to head into the locker room.

"Skye." Gail stopped me before I got to the door. "Sunny isn't doing the swimming lessons to surprise your mom, is he?"

I lowered my head and didn't say anything.

"I mean," Gail continued, "if it were a surprise, she wouldn't be coming to practice with him, right?"

I still didn't say anything.

"So all I can figure is that you lied to me about it. I hope you had a good reason to lie that way. I also hope that you know I don't like to hire people who have a tendency to avoid the truth."

I sighed and went back to the desk. "Gail, I'm sorry I lied. Sunny wanted the swimming lessons, and Mom wanted me to teach him. I didn't want to, because I have to spend so much time with him as it is, but Mom wouldn't take no for an answer. I thought this way we all got what we wanted. I didn't have to teach him, he still learned, and the pool got money for two sessions of lessons."

Gail arched an eyebrow. "Don't try to pretend that you did this for anyone but yourself, Skye. I put myself on the line by waiving the parent release signature because I trusted you."

"At least I didn't just forge her signature," I began. At Gail's glare I stopped and tried again. "My mom does want Sunny swimming," I protested.

"Not with my guards, though. She wants him swimming with you. There's a difference."

"Please don't tell, Gail," I pleaded.

She shook her head. "I'm not going to tell," she said simply. "But I'm not sure how long it's going to take you to earn my trust back. And as a prospective employee, that's not a good position to be in."

"I know. I'm sorry, Gail. Really, I am."

She just sighed. A couple of my teammates came in through the doors. I started to edge back toward the locker room doors.

"I'll make it up to you somehow. I promise."

As the locker room door shut behind me, she said, "Just remember that you really owe me now."

~

"...Yeah.... Okay.... You too.... Bye." I hung up the phone and buried my face in the sofa pillow, yelling in frustration. Four rejections in a row. Even though they all had valid reasons for saying no, I still didn't think I could make another phone call.

"Skye?" Sunny said.

I looked up. "Yeah?"

"What's wrong?"

"Nothing, Sunny. You done with your homework?"

He nodded.

"Cool."

He turned on the TV and sat down next to me on the sofa.

"Can you turn it down a little?" I asked. "I've got some phone calls to make."

"Who are you calling?" he asked as he turned the volume down.

"No one you know."

We were quiet for a few minutes. I had the phone in my hand, but I really didn't want to call anyone else.

Sunny was kind of squirming a little. I could tell he wanted to talk to me about something.

"What's up?" I hung up the phone, grateful for the excuse.

"Did you and Mike break up?"

The rumors at school must have really been flying. Even Sunny had heard about it.

"Yes."

He nodded and I could almost see the relief flood his face.

"You really didn't like him, did you?" I asked.

"He was mean."

"You said that before. But how was he mean? He never did anything to you, other than buy you a Happy Meal and let you ride in his car with us."

He bent his head down.

"Sunny?" Suddenly I had a bad feeling. "What did he do to you?"

"He was one of the big boys who used to shove me in the hall."

I was shocked. Last year, Sunny had had a real bad stretch of time for a few months. He was supposed to be mainstreamed as much as possible, and that meant he was out in the halls from time to time. Passing periods are fast moving, and a lot can happen in just a few moments. Some "big boys" had picked on Sunny, tripping or shoving him almost daily for a while. The time he came home with a black eye, Mom insisted that Sunny

tell her what had happened to him. She went to the school and pitched a
fit. The assistant principal found out who was involved and took care of
the problem. I never heard who the "big boys" were.

"Mike? Mike shoved and tripped you?"

He nodded.

"Why didn't you tell me before?"

"I was afraid to," he said simply. We were quiet for a minute, then he
said, "He did it again today."

My stomach was in vicious knots, and I almost ran for the bathroom.
I forced myself to swallow. My jaw was clenched. I could feel my temples
throbbing.

I looked at him. "Did you tell your teacher?"

"No."

"Sunny, you know you're supposed to tell as soon as that stuff happens, so it doesn't get out of hand like it did last year!"

He shrugged.

"If it happens again, you have to go tell. Promise me." If he said no, I
would have to report it instead, and Mike would probably deny it and say
I was trying to get back at him.

"Okay." He nodded.

The phone rang in my hand, making me jump.

"Hello?"

"Hey, how's it going?" Jenny asked.

"How's what going?" My mind was still on Sunny's problems.

"The phone calls, Skye. Any luck yet?"

I sighed. "Jenny, this is just awful. I don't think I can take much more
of this."

"Don't quit, Skye. We'll find someone."

"I'm not sure I want to," I said, taking the phone into the kitchen.

"What do you mean?"

"I mean…" I swallowed hard and dropped my voice so Sunny couldn't
hear. "I mean I don't think I can handle a date right now." I dreaded the
thought of being in the same room with Mike. But even worse, I realized
I was scared to be alone with any guy.

"Yes, you can," Jenny said firmly. "It'll be good for you to go out with someone nice. I'm not telling you to go out and get another boyfriend. I'm just saying you need to go to homecoming, and you need to go with a date." She paused. "Right?"

"Right," I said reluctantly.

"Okay, so who have you called?"

I gave her a rundown on the four I had called and their reasons to say no.

"So you've got three left, right?"

"Yeah."

She mentioned a couple more names that we had forgotten to add to the list. I wrote them down and hung up. Sunny was standing there watching me.

"What are you doing?" he asked.

"Nothing," I said.

"Why are you making so many calls?"

"Trying to find a date," I answered reluctantly.

"What for?"

"Homecoming."

"I thought the guys asked the girls."

I winced. He hadn't meant it the way it sounded, but it still hurt. "They do, usually. But since Mike and I just broke up, and homecoming is this weekend. I've got to find someone."

Jeff Miller was the next one on my list. He went to a different high school. Two years ago, he and I had been on the same summer swim team. We had called each other a few times that summer, and I had run into him at a party last year.

I forced myself to pick up the phone again and dial his number. "Hi, is Jeff there?... Hi, Jeff, it's Skye.... Yeah, it's been a while.... How are you doing?... Me too.... Have you taken the SATs yet?... I'm waiting for the January tests.... Yeah.... Hey, I know this is kind of short notice." I swallowed hard. This was my fifth call. It should have gotten easier, but it hadn't. "But I was wondering if you'd like to go to my homecoming dance with me.... This Saturday.... No, that's cool.... I understand.... Yeah, maybe next time.... Uh-huh.... You too.... Okay.... Bye."

I hung up the phone and looked at Sunny, who had been watching me the whole time. "You know," I told him, "this is hard enough without you staring at me."

"Did he say no, too?"

"Yes, he did."

"I'll take you."

For a minute I couldn't even understand what he had just said. "What?"

"I'll take you to homecoming."

I caught my laughter just in time. He was serious. "Sunny, I..."

His open big blue eyes were searching my face. "We could go to homecoming together. People go as friends, don't they?"

"Yes..." I hesitated.

He kept looking at me.

How was I supposed to get out of this without crushing him? "Sunny, that's really sweet, but...."

His lower lip was out again. "But you don't want to go with a retard."

"No! No, Sunny, that's not it at all! You're not a retard."

"Yes, I am."

"Sunny, I don't want to go with my brother, that's all." I hurried on, trying to explain. "You see, Mike's got a date already, so I have to have a date. I can't go with my brother, because that's not a real date."

He was staring at the TV.

"Sunny," I pleaded. "If Brad Pitt was my other brother, I couldn't go with him either. I've got to have a *real* date."

He got up. "Whatever. I'm going to go read."

"Sunny?"

He turned back around.

"Thank you. Really. It's really sweet of you to offer to go with your sister."

He just shook his head and kept walking toward his bedroom. I felt awful. I groaned again and fell back on the couch. I knew it hurt Sunny's feelings, but there was no way I could go with him. Mike would have too much fun with that. I stared at the phone, wishing it would just melt into the table.

About ten minutes later, the phone rang again.

"Hello?"

"Hi, is Skye there?" a familiar voice asked.

"This is she."

"Skye, this is Jeff."

I was surprised. "Oh, hi again."

"Hey, I know I just said I couldn't go to your dance, but after I got off the phone I started thinking about it. So I called work and got someone to switch shifts with me."

"Really?" I jumped up. "So you can go?"

"Yeah, if the offer is still open."

I was running in place, trying to keep from shouting with joy. "Oh, yes, the offer is still open. Thank you so much for doing that. That was really sweet of you."

"Well, it's been a long time since we swam together, but we always had fun."

"Yeah, we sure did. That's why I called you."

We talked for a few more minutes about the details. He would pick me up at 6:30 to go to dinner. I told him not to worry about a corsage for me, since I had asked him, but he said he wanted to get one anyway. I was afraid to bring up who was going to pay for dinner. I planned on paying for my meal. I would have to talk to Mom and see if I could get her to loan me some extra money, in case I needed to pay for both of us. We said good-bye.

"Yes!" I hollered, dancing around the room. "Oh, thank you!" I dialed Jenny's number.

"I got a date!" I yelled as soon as she picked up the phone.

"Who?"

"Jeff Miller."

"Which one was he?"

"He's one of my old swimming buddies."

"Oh, cool." Jenny sighed. "I'm so glad you found someone."

"You and me both." I flopped onto the couch, settling in for a long talk. Sunny's problems slipped from my mind.

CHAPTER TWELVE

The week was long and slow. I failed three quizzes because I couldn't concentrate on anything. I was very aware that people were talking about me.

I felt like a misfit. All I could see and feel was Mike pushing himself on me. I felt sick every time I saw Mike—or every time I looked at myself in the mirror, for that matter. I wondered what was wrong with me. Was I odd because I was still a virgin? Was it wrong to want it to be making love instead of just sex? To want to be with someone you knew would be in your life for a long time to come? What had I done to make Mike think I wanted to have sex with him?

Even some of my teammates were acting differently around me. Most of them gave me a quiet, unstated kind of support, but I knew a few of them were whispering behind my back. My lane mates were vocal about being on my side: they called Mike every name in the book on Monday and Tuesday, and began making up new ones on Wednesday. Between sets they would occasionally ask me a question, but I never answered them.

"You're not making this easy," Deb finally complained. "We've heard Mike's side but we don't know your story."

I adjusted my goggles and ignored her.

"We don't need to hear her story," Hannah said firmly.

I pushed off the wall and missed the rest of what was said.

The week or two before taper, we do the hardest workouts of the season. We would begin tapering the following week. Taper is the best part of the season because we have short, fast, and easy workouts. But for now, practices were brutal. I didn't mind, though. I needed it. And it got my mind off everything else for a little while.

I didn't let myself think of Mike during warm-up. I knew if I did, I'd go out too fast and run the risk of injury. After warm-up, though, I let him into my mind. Sometimes it seemed like the water sliding down my body was his hands, and it spurred me on to faster intervals. Other times I pretended my feet were kicking him or my hands were slapping him.

I cried and screamed underwater for more than half the sets, and pushed myself as hard as I could for every practice. I was exhausted afterward, but I still had trouble getting to sleep at night.

The only good thing about the week was that I barely saw Mike at all, and that was at a distance. Jenny made sure that everyone knew I had a hot date for homecoming and would not be sitting at home. I felt sorry for Jon, because Jenny pretty much told him that he couldn't talk to Mike anymore, but she wouldn't tell him the real reason.

Jon was waiting at our lockers Tuesday morning. I glanced around uncertainly.

"Hey, Jon. Looking for Jenny?"

"No, actually. I wanted to talk to you."

"Oh?" I tried not to look the way I felt, like a rabbit finding herself nose to nose with a fox.

"Mike's been talking a lot."

"I know."

"Jenny doesn't want me talking to him."

I didn't say anything.

"Mike's been my buddy since elementary school. I can't just quit being his friend without a reason."

I cleared my throat. "That's okay, I understand."

"Want to tell me what really happened?"

I started shaking my head before he even finished the question.

"I know he can be an ass, Skye."

A choked laugh escaped me. "Yeah," I said. "He can. I'll tell Jenny to get off your back."

"Or you could tell me what happened," he repeated. "Maybe I could help you."

"Thanks, Jon," I said. "I hope Jenny knows how lucky she is."

"Remind her of that, will ya? She always seems to forget." He grinned. "See ya later."

I shook my head as he walked away. Jon was such a nice guy. Jenny always seemed to get it all.

Later in the week, it *really* felt like Jenny had everything. On Thursday, she was named junior class princess. The senior class nominees would be presented at the game Friday night. Then the king and queen would be crowned at the dance on Saturday.

I decided not to go to the game on Friday. Sunny's cold had gotten worse again and I used that as an excuse.

⁓

Saturday morning, Sunny and I went swimming. Sandra said Sunny could definitely compete in the Special Olympics. I asked Sandra to get the entry forms. Sunny tried to say no, but I overruled him.

After lunch I tried to work on a project for American Lit. I stayed at it for about half an hour, then I gave up and went to my room. I pressed my dress and got out my shoes and purse. I called the restaurant to confirm our reservations. Mom had given me some money to help with dinner, but I was still afraid I wouldn't have enough to cover both dinners. I really hoped Jeff wouldn't mind going dutch.

Around four o'clock, I started getting ready. I took a long shower and let my hair air dry, long and loose around my shoulders. I painted my nails, and took extra care with my makeup.

I was ready at six. I hated being ready early, just sitting around and waiting, but I hated being late even more.

Sunny came out into the living room. "You look pretty."

"Thanks, Sunny. You going to be okay tonight?" Mom wouldn't be home until nine. She and I had argued about leaving Sunny by himself, but I had finally won when Sunny came in and said he wanted to stay home alone.

"Yeah."

"You know Mom's number is on the fridge."

He nodded.

"You know that you're not supposed to leave the house, and you're not supposed to answer the door."

He nodded again.

"Don't use the stove," I continued.

"Skye, I'm not a baby!" he protested.

I stopped. "I know. But if you want to be able to stay by yourself again, then you have to do everything right this time."

"I know," he said. "And I know what to do."

"Okay." I thought I heard a car, so I looked out the window. It wasn't Jeff. I turned back to Sunny. "Has Mike given you any more trouble?"

"No."

"Are you sure?" I pressed.

"I'm sure. I'm not a baby, Skye! I can take care of myself!"

"Okay, Sunny, I'm sorry." We sat there for a minute. "Did you get enough to eat?"

"Skye!"

"Okay, okay, I'm sorry, I'm sorry."

We were both quiet for a few minutes. "Hey! I forgot to ask Sandra the date for the Special Olympics."

"I'm not going."

"What do you mean?"

"I'm not going," he repeated stubbornly.

"Why not?"

For a long time he wouldn't say anything. Then, just when I was about to give up, he muttered something under his breath. "What?" I asked.

"They're November sixth."

I looked at Sunny across the table from me, head bent down, staring at the table. Now I knew why he hadn't told Mom about Special Olympics, why he had quit talking about them all the time.

"Oh," I said.

I was torn. I wanted Mom to see me at state. It hurt that she hadn't seen me compete since I was a freshman. But this would be Sunny's first meet ever. He had been working so hard. And I had done nothing to help him. I could help him now. He could go if Mom took him.

I stared at that shaggy blond head, but he wouldn't look up at me. I saw a tear fall and splatter on the table in front of him. That did it.

I sighed. "Sunny, we'll find a way for you to go to Special Olympics."

"How?" he asked without looking up. "You and Mom will be at your state meet."

"She can go to your meet instead."

"No!" He shook his head quickly. "She wants to see you swim."

"She wants to see you swim too."

"This is just my first meet," he said.

"I know. That's why she should be there."

He shook his head again. "No. Besides, I want to see you at state, too."

I was touched. He would give up a chance at the Special Olympics just to watch me.

"Sunny, we'll figure something out, I promise."

"How?" he demanded.

"I don't know," I admitted. "But we can figure something out. Maybe she could come to both."

Finally he looked up at me. "She could?"

"I'm not sure, but if Special Olympics are in the afternoon, she might be able to. Preliminaries are in the morning, early. I probably won't make it to the finals, and that's in the afternoon. "

"You'll win just like you always do." Sunny glared at me.

I didn't know how to respond to that. It was supportive in a way, and accusing in another.

"Well," I said, forcing cheer back into my voice, "there's no point getting all worried about it just yet. We still have plenty of time. Let's get the details and specifics on times for both events, and then we'll see what we can do. Okay?"

Sunny nodded. "Okay."

We sat there silently, watching TV, until Jeff came to pick me up.

As Jeff and I walked to the gym, I kept a hand pressed to my stomach, trying to calm the butterflies. I was terrified about going inside. What if everyone snubbed me? What if the first person I saw was Mike?

Jeff opened the gym door. Almost immediately, I heard a friendly voice call, "Skye!" Relief flooded through me.

"Hi, Jenny! You look great!" I gave her a hug.

"You do too! That dress looks wonderful on you!"

"Thanks," I said. "Jeff, this is my best friend, Jenny, and her boyfriend, Jon."

"Hi, Jeff. Nice to meet you," Jenny said, looking him up and down. She sized him up while he shook hands with Jon.

"How was your dinner?" I asked her.

"It was great. We had a lot of fun. I just wish we could have doubled for it."

I laughed. There was no way I could ever double with Jenny and Jon for dinner, because I could never afford where they went.

Jon and Jeff had apparently figured out that they knew each other from somewhere, and they were chatting to one side. Jenny took the opportunity to whisper in my ear.

"He's really cute!"

I grinned. "I know. And he's a real sweetheart, too. We've already had a fight tonight."

Dismay covered Jenny's face. "Oh, no! About what?"

"Paying for dinner. I wanted pay for it or at least to split it, since I had asked him. He wouldn't let me."

Jenny grinned. "I like him more and more."

We laughed. I scanned the gym nervously.

"Mike's not here yet," Jenny said in an undertone.

I nodded. "Good. I hope he and DeAnna get too busy and forget to come."

Giggling, Jenny said, "Me, too!" Glancing at Jeff, she whispered, "Does he know about Mike?"

I shook my head. "He asked me what happened to my other date. I told him that he had to go to a funeral."

"Too bad it wasn't his own," Jenny muttered.

The four of us wandered around for a little while. Jeff and I danced a few times, but neither of us were really into dancing, so we did more walking around and talking.

I found Hannah, and she was with Lou. I gave her a questioning look, and while Jeff and Lou talked, she told me that she had canceled her date with Jeremy. She didn't seem too worried about it, and I certainly couldn't criticize her. I was using Jeff almost the same way she had planned on using Jeremy.

Because of the year-round swimming circle, Jeff knew quite a few people at the dance, so he didn't feel left out at all. In fact, a couple of times we got into conversations with people I hardly recognized, but who were good friends with Jeff. I was having a great time, even though I had finally seen Mike and DeAnna from a distance. The timing was perfect, because I was giving Jeff a hug when I saw them. When Mike looked over at us, I hid my face in Jeff's shoulder, almost clinging to him to keep from collapsing to the floor. I told Jeff I wanted to sit down for a while, and we found some chairs near the wall.

At ten o'clock, the music stopped and a dramatic drumroll echoed through the gym. We stood up so we could see. Ms. Jenkins, who was chaperoning the dance, climbed up to the DJ's booth and took the microphone.

"Ladies and gentlemen, I hope you are all enjoying yourselves. I also hope that you enjoy the rest of the evening in a safe manner." Almost everyone groaned and a few made catcalls. "Mr. Mayville has asked me to present this year's homecoming court. Would you please come forward as I call your names?"

There was some general shuffling as she called out the names and people made way for them to approach the DJ booth. Ms. Jenkins turned to the side and picked up an envelope and a shiny cardboard crown.

"And now I'd like to announce this year's homecoming king…Mike Banner."

I closed my eyes as everyone else cheered. I took a half step back, right into Jeff.

He looked down at me. "You okay?"

I nodded and stayed there, leaning against him. He put his hands on my shoulders.

"And your homecoming queen is...DeAnna Garcia."

I closed my eyes again and opened them just in time to see Mike placing the cheesy-looking crown on DeAnna's head. Then he leaned forward and gave her a very deep kiss, in complete disregard of the school's policy against public displays of affection. Ms. Jenkins didn't say anything, but whether that was because she was in shock or too embarrassed, I couldn't tell. The DJ put on a slow song, and Mike and DeAnna started the dance.

"Would you like to dance?" Jeff asked into my ear.

"Huh?... Oh, thanks, but I...um...I have to go to the bathroom," I stammered. "I'll be right back."

I turned and tried to weave my way through the crowd. The song was almost halfway over by the time I got around to the other side of the gym. There were a lot of girls going in and out of the nearest bathroom, so I kept walking. Hoping I could find a less crowded bathroom, I headed down a dimly lit hallway. The sounds of the dance grew fainter. I went to the last bathroom before the metal gate that kept people from wandering through the whole building.

I was in luck. No one else was in the bathroom. I wanted desperately to splash cold water on my face, but that would wreck my makeup. So I took a paper towel and soaked in it cold water, then placed it on my forehead. I leaned against a wall and closed my eyes.

I couldn't believe the turn my life had taken. A week ago I thought I had it all: a popular boyfriend, good grades, a chance to be in the homecoming royalty, state qualifying times. Everything had seemed perfect. What happened to make it all go wrong? *Now my ex-boyfriend is in there dancing with the homecoming queen,* I thought, *while I'm in here with nothing.*

I looked in the mirror again. *I will survive,* I told myself. *In a few years, I'll have a hard time even remembering what Mike looked like. I don't need some guy to feel good about who I am. I'm tough, I'm smart, and I'm in control. It's time to get Mike out of my mind. So what if some people believe his lies? So what if I didn't get to be a homecoming princess? I still have state. No one can take that away from me.*

I re-wet the towel three times. Finally I felt pulled together enough to go back out to the dance. I felt guilty about how long I had left Jeff alone, but I just had to settle down before I went back out there.

When I stepped back out into the dim hallway, it took a minute for my eyes to adjust. I heard a girl's low, seductive chuckle and some whispering. Then DeAnna stepped out from one of the classroom doorways.

"I'll be right back," she said.

She hesitated when she saw me, but then she lifted her chin and strode past me, heading toward the bathroom.

Another shadow was in the doorway, and I knew it was Mike. I started to walk by, but he stepped out and blocked my path.

"Hey, Skye," he said.

I was determined to ignore him. I tried to go around him.

"What's the hurry?" he asked, stepping in front of me again. "I know you won't sleep with a guy, but I thought you could at least talk to a guy."

"Shut up, Mike, and get out of my way." My throat began to tighten up.

"Now, Skye," he said, "you almost sound upset with me."

"Oh, no," I retorted sarcastically. "Why would I be upset with you when you force yourself on me and then spread lies about me?"

"You know I didn't force you, Skye. You acted like you wanted it, and then when I got turned on, you panicked. I'm the one who should be upset."

"I don't have to listen to this. You're such a pathetic liar."

He tried to put his hands on my shoulders. I ducked out of the way, circling warily around.

"Come on, Skye. Why don't you come over to my house with DeAnna tonight? You don't have to do anything. I'll just show you what you're missing."

"You're disgusting, Mike. I don't know what I ever saw in you."

"No, no," he said. "You know you what you saw in me. The thing is, I don't know what I ever saw in a stuck-up prude like you."

"I am not a prude!" I turned to walk away. My face was burning.

He laughed. "If you really don't think you're a prude, then you're just as retarded as that reject of a brother you—"

"What?" I spun back around.

"You heard me."

"You leave Sunny alone, Mike!" This time I was the one advancing on him. My fists were clenched at my sides.

"Ooh, scary. Sticking up for a retard. Real touching."

"He's not the retarded one, Mike. *You* are. I can't believe you'd pick on him." My temples were pounding.

"What's wrong with your mom, Skye? You're a prude, your brother's retarded, so there must be something wrong with your mom, too. I guess that's why your dad left. The three of you are rejects."

Before I even had time to think, I was throwing a wild punch at his face. He didn't see it coming, and I connected solidly on his jaw, knocking him back into the lockers. Excited, I went for another punch with my left hand. This time he ducked. My hand connected with the lockers and exploded in pain.

Mike's shocked, angry look faded and he started to laugh.

I turned and ran down the hall, trying to escape. My hand was killing me. Tears were threatening. I had spent all that time pulling myself together, and now I was going back into the gym a bigger mess than I had been when I left it.

Biting back the tears, I found Jenny and Jon almost immediately.

"Where have you been?"

"Have you seen Jeff?" I asked, trying to keep my voice from quavering.

They looked at me in confusion. "He was looking for you. When we couldn't find you, he got upset. I tried to tell him you wouldn't ditch him, but I guess he didn't believe me," Jenny said.

"I think he might have left already," Jon said uncertainly.

"Jon, could you please go look for him?" I asked.

"Um…" Jon hesitated, but then Jenny gave him a pointed look. "Sure, Skye, I'll go find him for you."

As soon as Jon was out of earshot, Jenny turned to me anxiously. "Skye, what happened? We were looking all over for you. Are you okay?" She guided me toward an empty chair.

I was holding my arm up across my stomach, trying not to think of the throbbing pain. I felt sick, dizzy, and my knees wouldn't stop shaking. I grinned weakly. "I ran into Mike."

Her eyes got big. "Oh, no! What happened?"

"He was a jerk," I said simply. I leaned my head back and closed my eyes, hoping the tears would stay in my eyes.

"He was himself," she said.

"Yeah."

"What happened to your arm?"

"My hand," I corrected. "I kind of punched him."

She began to grin. "Hard enough to hurt your hand?"

"Well, yeah, but I hit him with the other hand."

Jenny frowned in confusion. "Huh?"

"I went to hit him again and he ducked. My left hand met the locker door instead."

"Oh, no! Let me see it."

I shook my head and leaned back. "No. I'll be all right. I just need to go home and put some ice on it." I took a quick look around. "I don't want to hurt Jeff's feelings, though."

"He'll understand. If you just tell him you punched out your ex-boyfriend and broke your hand, I think he'll take you home. He won't want to run the risk of making you mad." She laughed, but I just took a deep breath and tried to focus on the pain. If I concentrated, maybe I could keep the pain from spreading. My hand was already red and swelling rapidly.

Jon came back about five minutes later. "I can't find him."

"Wonderful," I muttered.

Jenny and Jon decided that they would take me home, and then come back and look for Jeff some more. We walked out to the parking lot. Jeff was in his car, backing out.

"Where were you?" he asked. "I thought you had ditched me."

"I'm really sorry," I said lamely. "I didn't realize I was gone so long."

Jenny broke in. "She hurt her hand. We were going to take her home."

"I can take you," Jeff said, looking at me. "Unless you'd rather go with them?"

"I'd really appreciate a ride home, Jeff," I said. "Thanks, Jenny and Jon. I'll be all right now." I opened the car door.

"Are you sure you're okay?" Jenny asked.

I bit my lip and tried to grin. "Sure. I'm fine."

"You're looking really pale."

"I'm in a lot of pain," I said.

"We should probably just take you to the hospital."

"No!"

Jenny looked at me. "You're going to tell your mom that you need to go to the doctor, right?"

I took a long quivering breath. "I'm fine. I'm sure it's just badly bruised. I don't need to go to the doctor."

"Let me see your hand."

"No." I shook my head and pulled my hand in even closer to my body for protection as I got into Jeff's car.

"You need to see a doctor, Skye, just to check," Jenny said as Jon led her back to the school.

Stubbornly, I shook my head. "I'll call you tomorrow," I said. "Let's go, Jeff."

We were quiet on the way home. When we got to my house, he offered to come inside with me.

"No, thanks, Jeff. I feel terrible that I ruined the evening."

"Don't worry about it. I hope your hand isn't broken or anything. Call me and let me know how things go."

"I will," I promised as I climbed out of the car.

CHAPTER THIRTEEN

I pushed the front door open carefully, still cradling my left arm against my body. Mom and Sunny were sitting on the couch watching a movie. They both turned around when I came in.

"What did you rent?" I asked, trying to divert their attention. I bit the inside of my bottom lip as I lowered my left hand and let it dangle at my side. I was hoping it looked natural, and I was also hoping Mom couldn't see the swelling from where she was.

"*Star Trek IV,*" Mom said, looking at her watch. "What're you doing home so early?"

I shrugged. "The dance was kind of boring, and my date and I didn't get along as well as I thought we would. He has to get up early tomorrow, so we decided to call it a night."

I headed for the kitchen.

"Great!" Sunny called. "You can watch the rest of the movie with us. Mom also got *Star Trek V.*"

I opened the freezer door and scooped ice into a glass. Then I grabbed a Diet Coke from the fridge. It took me a minute to figure out how to carry the can and the glass with one hand. Finally I stacked the glass on top of the can, and wrapped my right hand around them both at the middle.

"Thanks, Sunny, but I'm kind of tired," I said, holding my left hand behind me as I walked through the living room. "I think I'll just go curl up in bed with a book and then go to sleep."

"I understand we have a problem," Mom said.

It felt like my heart stopped at the same time my feet did. "What do you mean?"

"I told her about the Special Olympics," Sunny said.

"Oh, that," I said slowly as my heart started again. "Yeah, we'll have to figure something out." I started toward my room again.

"Do you have any suggestions?"

"Not really. I might once I see what the schedules are for both of them. I'll try to get the information this week. Good night," I added, trying to end the conversation.

Mom was looking at me funny. "Are you sure you're okay?"

"Yeah. I'm just tired, and a little bummed things didn't go the way I thought they would."

"Skye, I'm sorry. I know this has been hard on you—breaking up with Mike just before the dance and all. But things'll work out for you. Being crowned princess is not that big of a deal. You have so much to feel good about: your grades, your swimming, your wonderful personality—"

"I know, Mom," I said, cutting her off.

She looked at me. "Something's going on." She patted the cushion next to her. "Come on, sit down and tell your mommy everything."

I forced a laugh and shook my head. "Really, Mom, I'm tired and I just want to go to sleep."

She sighed. "Okay, but I expect a full report tomorrow morning."

"Deal," I said, knowing there was no way I was going to give her a "full report."

Getting undressed was awful. Every time I bumped my hand or even touched it, I had to fight to keep from crying out. My left index and middle fingers and my thumb were all swollen to twice the size of my right fingers. Plus, my palm was bleeding where my fingernails had been driven into the skin. My whole hand was throbbing and felt like it was on fire.

It took me almost five minutes to get most of the makeup off my face, since I could only use one hand. I didn't bother trying to brush my hair. After I brushed my teeth, I took three ibuprofen tablets.

Once in my room, I shut the door behind me and looked in my closet for a plastic bag. I couldn't find one. Tears were running down my face. My hand hurt even when I wasn't moving. Then I spied my swimming bag. I pulled out my swim cap and dumped the ice into it. I bit hard on my lip when I put the cap on my hand.

I sat down on my bed, absolutely exhausted, both emotionally and physically. I just sat there, not moving at all, not even thinking. Somehow the physical pain had dulled the emotional pain. By the time I came out of the daze, most of the ice had melted. My hand was still swollen, now an angry red, and it was still throbbing.

I got up, went to the kitchen, dumped the water down the drain, and got some more ice. Then I went back to my room and curled up under the blankets, hoping that I could drift off to sleep and not feel the pain for a while.

An hour later, I was still awake and the pain had not decreased at all. I knew I couldn't just lie there any longer. I got up and looked down the hall. There was still a light coming from under Mom's bedroom door. I went back into my room and carefully pulled on a sweatshirt and sweatpants.

Quietly I padded down the hall to my mom's room, cradling my injured hand in front of me. I knocked gently with my elbow.

"Yes?" she said.

I pushed the door open and went in. "Um, Mom?"

She put down the book she was reading. "Skye, what's wrong? You're awfully pale."

"I think I need to go to the hospital," I said.

"What's wrong?" she asked, sitting up in alarm.

"I think I broke my hand."

She threw back the covers and started to get out of bed. "You what?"

"I think I broke my hand."

She came across the floor to me, looking at my hand. "How?"

"It's a long story."

Mom reached for my hand and I pulled back. "Skye, I have to see it," she said.

"Mom, it really hurts." I was crying again.

"You have to let me see it," she repeated patiently.

"Don't touch it!" I moaned. I held my swollen, discolored hand out in front of me.

She shook her head. "Okay, let's go get Sunny."

"Why?"

"So we can take you to the emergency room."

"We don't need to drag him with us. Let him sleep."

She looked at me and then went to the closet, getting her shoes and a pair of jeans. "Okay, you go tell him what's going on and if he wants to stay here, he can. I'll meet you by the door in a minute."

I nodded and went back down the hall to Sunny's room.

"Sunny?" I said softly, opening his door.

He mumbled something and turned in his bed.

"Sunny!" I said louder.

"What?" he groaned.

"Listen, Mom and I have to go somewhere. You can stay here and sleep if you want to."

He didn't say anything.

"Sunny?"

"What?"

"Do you want to stay and sleep or do you want to go with me and Mom?"

"Sleep," he mumbled.

"Okay." I pulled his door shut and then went to get my shoes.

Mom was waiting for me at the door. She had a bag of ice wrapped in a towel. "Here."

I took it without a word and followed her out to the car.

During the trip to the hospital, Mom asked me again what had happened to my hand.

"I hit a locker."

"When?"

"Tonight."

"At the dance?"

I nodded. Mom was quiet for a few minutes. I knew she was trying to get her questions in order.

"Why did you wait until now to tell me? No, let's see…you must have waited because you didn't want me to know," she reasoned out loud. "So, what I need to know first is how did you hit the locker?"

I leaned my head against the window. "I was trying to hit Mike."

"And you missed," Mom said dryly.

"Not the first time," I said quickly. "He ducked the second shot."

Mom was quiet again. "Why did you hit him?"

"I don't want to talk about it."

Mom started to laugh. "Oh, my poor, confused Skye. That's no longer an option. You see, I'm going to be paying for the treatment of this injury, and therefore I get to know why I'm paying for it."

I was quiet. Mom sighed.

"You're a bright girl, Skye, and for the most part you're reasonable. I don't think you would just haul off and hit somebody."

"I wouldn't."

"So he did something."

I didn't answer.

"Please tell me it wasn't just that he was in the homecoming royalty and you weren't."

"No, Mom, that wasn't it."

"So tell me. Instead of making me guess all these wrong answers, just tell me. I'm going to find out."

"We had a big fight last weekend."

"And you broke up. I knew that."

"He's been saying stuff about me at school."

"And?"

I shook my head. "He just made me mad."

"Not good enough, Skye."

We were almost at the hospital.

"What did he do to make you break up with him?"

"I don't want to talk about it."

Mom shook her head and I could feel her frustration radiating off her in waves. We were pulling into the parking lot. "Well, understand this. We're going to take care of your hand right now, and I am sorry you're hurt. But you're grounded until I get a satisfactory explanation for all this."

"Mom, that's not fair!"

"No, it's not, but neither is life. I have a right to know what's going on, Skye. I've always trusted you and I thought you trusted me—trusted me enough to talk to me." I could hear the hurt in her voice.

There was nothing I could say. I trusted her, but I didn't want to talk about my personal life. Right now it was too embarrassing, too painful. I knew she wanted to be involved in my life, but the truth was, she wasn't. It wasn't because she didn't care; it was simply because she had too much to do.

Neither of us said anything until we got to the emergency room desk. Then we answered the questions and filled out forms. We waited in silence in the waiting room for about a half hour. Then the nurse came and took us back to a room.

They x-rayed my hand and found fractures in three bones. It wasn't until they started putting the cast on my hand that it dawned on me what this could mean.

"Wait," I said, stopping the doctor. "How long do I have to wear this cast?"

"Six weeks," he said.

I shook my head. "Uh-uh, no way. I can't."

He raised his eyebrows at me. "You can't?" he asked.

"I have the state swim meet in two weeks," I said.

He whistled. "Well, I'm sorry, but we have to immobilize your entire hand. The only way we can do that is with a cast."

"Is it waterproof? Can I swim with it?"

"We have some that are waterproof, but they're a lot more expensive," he said hesitantly. "You couldn't do much swimming in one anyway, I'm afraid."

I didn't have to look at Mom to know she was shaking her head.
There was no point in asking. We couldn't afford an expensive waterproof
cast. The doctor exchanged a look with my mom.

"Could I just wear a splint?" I pleaded. "One that I could get wet?"

"The purpose of a cast is to keep your hand and wrist from moving,
so the muscles won't pull on the bones," he explained in a gentle tone.
"There's too much movement involved in swimming to set this with a
splint and let you get in the water. Just entering the water from a dive
could be dangerous, and each pull would be a huge strain. We have to use
a cast to immobilize it completely."

I hung my head and cried while he finished the cast. Mom rubbed my
back and made soothing sounds, but I didn't get any comfort from her
sympathy. I had worked so hard, and now I couldn't go. At that moment,
I hated Mike more than I thought it was possible to hate anyone.

〜

When I woke up late the next morning, I was groggy. The painkillers the
doctor had given me had put me out on the way home. I could sort of
remember Mom waking me up so I could stumble out of the car and
down the hall to my room, but I didn't remember much else.

I looked at my cast. My hand was throbbing again, but it was a dis-
tant, dull throb. It didn't hurt nearly as bad as knowing I couldn't go to
state. Just thinking about state made me feel sick.

Sighing deeply, I shoved the blankets off me and went to the bathroom. Learning how to shower with one hand was a new challenge. I
wrapped the cast with a plastic grocery bag and then tried to keep it out
of the direct flow of water. The shower took longer than usual, but I
managed. Getting the shampoo out of my hair was the hardest part.

I wandered out to the living room. Sunny was already there, watching
TV. He said hi, and then did a double take.

"What did you do to your hand?"

"I broke it."

"How?" His brow was furrowed with concern.

"I hit a locker," I said, shaking my head.

"What did you do that for?"

"That's exactly what I want to know," Mom said from the kitchen doorway. "So let's talk."

I groaned. "Mom, I just woke up."

"Perfect timing, then. It will all be fresh in your mind."

"Haven't I suffered enough?" I pleaded. "I mean, don't you think not being able to go to state is enough of a punishment?"

"No," Mom said. At the same time Sunny said, "Why can't you go to state?"

I chose to address Sunny, which turned out to be a mistake. "I can't swim with a cast."

"Oh, no!" Sunny looked really upset. "I'm sorry."

"Thanks, Sunny," I said.

"Sunny, this also means she's not going to be able to give you swimming lessons anymore. We'll have to see if we can find someone else to teach you so you can go to the Special Olympics."

Sunny and I looked at each other. I bit my lip and thought for a moment, then said, "I know who we can get to teach Sunny until Special Olympics."

"I figured you would," Mom said. "Do you think you could get someone to work with him every day for the next two weeks, instead of just three days a week?"

Sunny said, "No, because that's not how the lesson schedule works."

Mom smiled. "Those are the group lessons, Sunny. I'm talking about private lessons for you."

"But I want to keep thwimming with Thandra!"

I closed my eyes. It was out.

"What do you mean?"

Sunny didn't say anything. He was staring at me with huge eyes, suddenly aware that he had told.

There was nothing for me to do now, except explain everything. I cleared my throat. "Sunny's been taking group lessons," I tried to say. It came out a weak whisper.

Mom turned to me. "What?"

"I enrolled Sunny in group lessons."

The whole house was quiet. I felt pinned to the wall with Mom's stare.

"You mean," Mom said slowly, "you haven't been teaching Sunny lessons? You put him in group lessons instead?"

I couldn't say anything, so I simply nodded.

Mom laughed, but it was an empty laugh. "You have no idea how grounded you are right now. You had better start speaking quickly. I want the whole truth, from the beginning."

I sank down onto the floor, leaning against the wall. Staring at a spot on the carpet, I told Mom everything that had happened in the last month, right up until the weekend I broke up with Mike.

"I don't know what to think, Skye. I've always been able to depend on you. What's going on? You lie to me, you won't talk to me. What's wrong?"

Afraid to look up, I just shrugged. "I'm sorry," I mumbled.

"Is that all you've got to say?"

I nodded, keeping my eyes on the floor.

She sighed. "How much did these lessons cost?"

"Fifty dollars," I said.

"Fine. And how much have I already paid you to teach Sunny? You owe me all of that money. You can either work it off next semester by teaching Sunny lessons or I can take it out of your allowance. And you will continue to take him to the lessons that he's in, but you'll do so without the car." She paused. "I forgot. You can't drive now anyway."

When I didn't respond, Mom got up. "Sunny, do you want to go to the pool?"

His eyes still huge and troubled, Sunny looked at me.

I sighed and looked up at him. "Sunny, it's okay. This isn't your fault. Go practice."

He got up slowly and went down the hall to get his swimming stuff.

Mom headed toward her room. "You have to stay here, Skye," she said over her shoulder. "You're grounded for the rest of the month."

All things considered, I felt I was getting off easy.

I went to my room to get a book to read, and as I came back into the living room, I overheard Mom talking on the phone with my coach. She told him the doctor said I couldn't swim. I waved my good arm frantically in the background, trying to get her attention. She ignored me until she got off the phone.

"What?" she demanded.

"Mom," I groaned. "Now I have to have doctor's permission to get in the water."

She looked at me funny. "You're not getting in the water, remember? The doctor said that you were out until the cast comes off. You can't get it wet."

"What about putting a plastic bag over it?"

"Skye." Mom was shaking her head. "You couldn't race with that cast on anyway."

"But, Mom, can't I just try? See if it really hurts that bad to swim?"

"Skye, we're not just talking about temporary pain. We're talking about possible permanent damage."

"But, Mom!"

"Honey, I know this is hard, but you're going to have to accept it. I'm sure you'll make state again next year."

"But, Mom!"

"No buts about it, Skye. You can't swim till the cast is off. End of discussion." She picked up the car keys. "Sunny, are you ready to go?"

After they left, I wandered around the house for a while like I was lost, which was how I felt. Then, to keep my mind occupied, I folded the laundry the best I could with one hand and put everything away. I hung up Alison's dress and put it back in the bag. I even vacuumed the carpet in the hallway and the living room, but my mind was still racing. I couldn't figure out what I had done so wrong that would cause my life to end up like this. I kept thinking about what Mike had said last night. I tried to replay scenes with him in my mind, trying to figure out if I had done something to make him act that way. I couldn't see anything, but I knew it must be there.

Finally, I called Jenny. I worked very hard at keeping my voice steady. But when I told her I wouldn't be able to swim at state, I burst into tears anyway.

"Well," Jenny said, "I think I have some news that will make you feel better."

"What? I could really use it."

"Well, after you left, Jon and I went back to the dance. And I went looking for Mike."

"Why?"

"Because I wanted to let him know exactly what I think of him."

"Jenny," I groaned, "I don't think this is going to make me feel any better."

"Hang on, give me a chance to finish, okay? So I find him, and, girl, you put one heck of a hit on him."

"I knew that."

"No, I mean, it was already turning blue. Everyone was asking what had happened to him."

"And this is supposed to make me feel better?"

"Would you let me finish?"

"Sorry," I said.

"Anyway, he was trying to ignore it and make up some stupid story about running into something," she said.

"Like my fist," I muttered.

"But then DeAnna comes out and tells the whole story."

"She what? What do you mean? She doesn't even know the whole story!"

"Okay, okay, but she must have overheard some of it. She saw you deck him."

"Really?"

"Yeah. So she spilled the beans." I could tell Jenny was grinning.

"I don't know," I said slowly. "Now I almost think I need to be grateful that DeAnna is alive. That will be a big adjustment for me."

"You should really be glad she's alive."

"Well, yeah, cause she blew Mike's cover."

"Well, that and the fact that she ditched him."

"She did what?"

Jenny was giggling. "I knew it would make you feel better. Apparently, DeAnna decided she needed to score with someone new. Someone who didn't get beaten up by junior girls. She left with Jim Shive."

I was laughing too. "He got ditched! Oh, that is so cool."

"He got hit and *then* he got ditched. I think it was a good evening for him."

We laughed.

"Skye?"

"What?"

"I really think you should tell people what happened. You know, so he can take the rap for being a bastard, instead of you taking the rap for something you never did."

My insides flipped over. "I don't know," I said doubtfully. "I must have done something wrong."

"Stop it, Skye. Just stop it right there. You did not do anything wrong. You and I had even talked about it before it happened. You were very up front with him about your expectations. He was the jerk who did something wrong. Not you. You did nothing wrong. Don't even start blaming yourself."

I was quiet.

"Skye? I need to hear you say that you don't blame yourself for this."

"Okay, Jenny." I sighed. "It wasn't my fault."

"Whose fault was it?"

"Mike's." My voice was stronger that time.

"Okay. Now back to my first point. I think we need to tell the world what a horse's backside he really is."

"Jenny," I said, shaking my head. "It's just not worth it, okay? I just want to forget I ever spent time with him or cared what he thought."

"Okay," Jenny said with an I'll-go-along-with-it-for-you tone in her voice.

I sighed. "I guess I should call Jeff and apologize."

"Ugh," Jenny said. "Doesn't sound like much fun, but you're probably right."

"I'll talk to you later," I said. "If I don't make this call now, I never will."

"Okay," Jenny said. "Oh, by the way…"

"Yeah?"

"After Jon and I left the dance, we went to Denny's."

"And?"

"Well, Steve was working there."

"Tell me you didn't do anything."

"Okay, if that's what you really want," Jenny said. I knew she was smiling again.

"What did you do?"

"You just said you didn't want me to tell you!"

"Jenny!"

She chuckled. "You might get a phone call, that's all."

"What did you do? Jenny, you better tell me!"

"He just mentioned that he had heard you and Mike broke up, and was wondering if it was true. I told him it was. He seemed pretty happy to hear it."

"That's all you said?"

"That's it."

"Okay, Jenny, I'm going to believe you."

"Well, you should." Jenny said. "I've got to get going,"

"Me, too."

"I'm really sorry about your hand, Skye."

"Thanks."

"Bye."

"Bye."

I sat there staring at the phone for about ten minutes, trying to figure out exactly what to say to Jeff. How do you explain to someone that you used him? Finally I took a deep breath, picked up the phone, and dialed his number.

I got his answering machine.

"Hi, Jeff, this is Skye…um…. I wanted to tell you I had a really great time at dinner last night. And the dance was fun too. Sorry we had to leave early, but as it turns out, I did break some bones in my hand. If you want all the details, just call me. Thanks again. Hope to talk to you soon."

I hung up the phone feeling like a total loser.

After I calmed down a little, I wandered into my room and tried to do some homework. I still couldn't concentrate for very long.

Mom and Sunny came back around five. They had rented another movie, so we spent the evening watching it. Mom made dinner, and we ate in the living room in front of the TV. It was a pretty lazy evening for all of us. But it wasn't relaxing for me. Every time Mom looked at me or said my name, I tensed up, expecting her to ask me about Mike.

I went to bed at my usual time. I had just gotten settled in when there was a knock at the door.

"Come in," I called, expecting it to be Sunny with some homework he had forgotten to do.

It was Mom. She came in and sat down on the edge of my bed.

"Thanks for folding the clothes," she said. "How are you feeling?"

"Depends on what you mean."

"How's your hand?"

I shrugged. "It's all right. The painkillers seem to be working."

"How's the rest of you?"

"Tired." I looked down at my cast. "Feeling guilty. Feeling rotten because I can't swim. Not looking forward to telling people I broke my hand hitting a locker."

"I'm glad you're feeling guilty," Mom said. "That means you have a conscience. Skye, I would like to know why you lied to me like that."

"I guess I was just sick of always being around Sunny. I got tired of taking him everywhere. I wanted to have a life of my own."

"Skye, I'm sorry our family situation has been so difficult. I wish a lot of things had been different. I know you do a lot around here, a lot more than most girls your age, and I know I have a lot of high expectations for you." She reached over and pushed my hair back behind my ear. "But you have even higher expectations for yourself. I worry that you push yourself too hard. You try to be perfect in everything you do, all of the time. It's okay to be human and make mistakes."

That was nice to hear, but it wasn't much comfort. She didn't know everything yet.

We were both quiet for a few moments. Then Mom frowned. "Do you know how much Sunny looks up to you?"

I sighed.

"He's your brother, Skye. And believe it or not, someday you'll discover how important the time is that you spend with your family."

I didn't say anything.

She shook her head. "I know he's not the easiest person in the world to deal with, but frankly, my dear, neither are you."

"I know," I muttered.

"We all have things in life that are hard, and they either break us or make us better. It's your choice." She looked at me. "Remember, he's the only brother you get to have."

"I know," I repeated. "And I do care, it's just that—"

"There are times you'd like to have more time to yourself," she finished for me.

"Exactly."

"I do my best to give you some free time. I know you don't think it's enough, but it's all I can give you right now. And you're going to get more time, Skye. You're not that far away from moving out and being on your own." She sighed. "Being an adult is not always all you think it's going to be. It gets lonely. It's nice to have someone who will always be there. That's what your family is." She paused for a moment. "You know, we both could learn a lot from Sunny."

I looked at her in disbelief.

"It's true. Sunny is forgiving and accepting of people. He loves you no matter what you say or do. It doesn't matter to him that you're not really perfect, because in his eyes you are perfect. If there were more people like Sunny, the world would be a much nicer place."

I sighed again and absorbed her words in silence.

"Are you ready to tell me what happened with you and Mike?" Mom asked gently.

I was tired, and I knew she wasn't going to leave until she had the information she wanted. I waited a few moments and chose my words carefully. "He wanted more from me than I was ready to give," I said finally.

She tilted my chin up and searched my face. "Did he try to take what he wanted?"

I shifted uncomfortably.

"Skye? Did he rape you?" I heard the panic enter her voice.

"No!"

"Are you sure?"

"Mom, I think I'd know if I'd been raped."

"I mean, are you sure you're not just covering for him?"

"I'm sure. He wouldn't take no for an answer, so I had to get his attention."

"How did you do that?"

"With my knee."

Mom took a deep breath and shook her head slowly. "You know, Skye, I'm beginning to think you've got a violent streak," she said.

I laughed. "Just when it comes to a jerk named Mike."

"Do you feel like telling me the whole story, Skye?" she asked, hesitating. "I know it may be a little embarrassing or uncomfortable for you, but I need to know exactly what happened between you two."

So, slowly, I told her everything, including the part about Mike picking on Sunny. When I finished, I said, "See? So it's not really a big deal."

She looked at me with big, sad eyes. "It *could* have been. I'm furious about what he did to you, and I think he owes you a huge apology. But what's more, if something isn't done now, it might very well end up being rape for his next girlfriend."

I looked at her. "I hadn't thought of it that way."

She nodded. "It's not an easy thing to talk about, but by staying quiet about it, you're helping him continue this behavior. And the way he treated Sunny just shows there is a pattern here."

I had a sinking feeling in my stomach. "What are you going to do?"

Mom took a deep breath. "We should press charges—"

"No!"

Mom looked at me out of the corner of her eye. "Well, at the very least, I'm going to call his parents."

"No, Mom, please! It won't do any good. He'll just deny it."

"Skye, I'm sorry. But his parents need to know, so they can talk to him and help him understand that what he did was wrong. From what you've said about his actions and what he's doing at school, I'm not sure he knows that. I'm going to call not just for you and not just for the girl who might be next, but for Mike too. He's running the risk of getting into really deep trouble if he doesn't shape up."

"But what if his parents don't believe you? What if they just take Mike's side?"

"I know that's a possibility, but I still think we have to try."

I groaned and slipped down under my blankets. "I'll never be able to show my face again."

Mom moved the blanket off my face and kissed my cheek. "My guess is that he's the one who won't want to show his face."

She got up to leave.

"Mom?"

She turned around.

"Am I still grounded?"

Laughing, she said, "Oh, yes, absolutely."

"Mom?"

"Hmmm?"

"I love you."

"I love you, too, honey. Good night."

I looked at the clock. Maybe she would think it was too late to call tonight, and then tomorrow she'd forget. Maybe.

CHAPTER FOURTEEN

I dreaded going to school on Monday.

Fortunately, it went a lot better than I thought it would. Jenny said most of the people she talked to had heard that I had punched Mike, and they were now beginning to think that maybe he had lied about our situation. Very few people mentioned Mike to me, and no one asked me about my cast. I guess they just assumed I had broken my hand on his face. The thought made me laugh.

Steve was waiting for me outside of Government. We chatted a little, and during class he passed me another note.

Skye—

I'm really sorry about your hand. I know you were looking forward to state. I'm also sorry I didn't make it to one of your meets this year. I'll come next year and watch you qualify early in the season! Anyway, I was wondering if you were interested in going to a movie sometime? (You never did answer me before!)

Steve

His note made me smile, really smile, for the first time in what felt like forever. I started to write him back, but had a hard time with the wording. I didn't finish in time to give him the note before the bell rang. I told him on the way out of class that I would give it to him during art.

But I didn't make it to art class. After lunch, I got called down to the counselor's office instead. I thought Sunny was having another problem.

When I walked in, Mike was there. I almost backed out of the room. The counselor, Mr. Bond, stopped me and asked me to sit down. I glanced over at Mike. He looked angry.

I stared at Mr. Bond in utter confusion.

"You did know your mother called the Banners last night, right?"

I sank in the chair and closed my eyes. "She said she was going to, but I was hoping she hadn't."

Mr Bond looked at me with concern. "I know this must be difficult for you. But I've talked to both of your parents, and we all feel that if we don't deal with what has happened, then it may continue to affect the two of you at school.

I was staring at the floor. I knew that if I looked up I would either start crying or try to hit Mike again.

"Do you know what your mom talked to the Banners about?"

"Yeah," I mumbled.

"Can you tell me, in your own words, what happened?"

I looked at Mr. Bond in horror. I had barely been able to tell my mother, and now he wanted me to talk to him about it? In front of Mike?

Without warning, the tears were threatening. I had become a regular rain cloud in the last week and it was driving me crazy.

"Everyone in here knows her version of what happened," Mike snapped. "We don't need to go through it again."

"Her version? You don't agree with what Skye's mother told your parents?"

"It doesn't matter. My parents believed her. My dad busted me for it pretty hard."

"What don't you agree with?" Mr. Bond asked.

"I haven't done anything wrong! She wanted it! Then she changed her mind!"

I couldn't stand it. "What made you think I wanted it?" I blurted out. "When I told you weeks ago in the mall that we weren't going to have sex? When I asked you to stop? When I *screamed* at you to stop? When I drove my knee into your crotch? Which of those did you think was a come-on?"

Mike slouched back down in his chair, muttering. Mr. Bond pushed a box of Kleenex toward me. I hadn't realized I was crying again.

"Mike's parents wanted him to apologize to you," he said. "They were afraid you wouldn't want to talk to him alone, so they called me to arrange it."

Suddenly, Mike said in a toneless voice, "I'm sorry for what I did. And I'm sorry for what I said, last week and at the dance Saturday. It won't happen again." I glanced at him. He was staring at the floor, reciting from memory. There was absolutely no emotion in his voice. He half-sighed, half-groaned. "My parents also want you to know they're going to put me in counseling to help me understand what I did."

I nodded. I knew it wasn't a real apology. He hadn't looked at me, and clearly he still didn't think he had done anything wrong. But strangely, for the first time, I truly felt that he was the one to blame.

"You also need to apologize to Sunny," I said.

Mike slunk down further in his chair.

Mr. Bond looked at me. "Was Sunny there?"

"No," I said. "But Mike's been picking on him ever since."

"Picking on him how?"

I looked at Mike. He glared at me and then turned to Mr. Bond.

"I just kind of gave him a little push a couple times in the hall during passing period," he said, shrugging to show it wasn't any big deal.

Mr. Bond scowled and wrote something down. Then he sighed and looked back up at Mike. "That just makes one more thing we need to talk about," he said.

Mike shrugged again, looking around the office.

"Skye, I think I can promise you that Sunny won't be harassed by Mike anymore." he said. "Can you both accept this and let it end here?"

We both nodded.

"Okay. Skye, Ms. Jones will write you a pass. Mike, we need to discuss a few more things."

I got up, happy to leave. Mr. Bond walked me to the door of his office.

"Skye?" Mr. Bond said. "You may need to talk to someone about what's happened. Please come in whenever you need to, or you can talk to any of our other counselors."

I nodded again and got out of the room as fast as I could. I guess I looked pretty upset, because Ms. Jones asked me if I was all right. I told her I'd be fine if I could have a little time to get myself together. She wrote me a library pass so I wouldn't have to go straight to class. I went to my locker, and then to the library.

I found a study carrel in the back and sat down. Then I spent a few minutes finishing the note for Steve. I tried to explain what I'd been through, but it didn't sound right. I started over and said that I would love to go see a movie with him but that I was grounded for the month. Then I told him I wanted to talk to him before we went because I needed to explain some things. I signed my name and put my phone number under it.

Then I put my head down and stayed in the library for the rest of the half hour, just thinking and breathing deeply.

∽

After I told Mom about the meeting with Bond, she decided that being grounded for two weeks would be enough. But those two weeks were long and slow.

It was hard to cook with one hand in a cast, so I had to teach Sunny. We spent a lot of time in the kitchen together, and I found myself telling him about my days. He told me all about his days too.

"I want to cook something besides macaroni," he said one night.

I raised my eyebrows. "Getting a little ahead of yourself, aren't you?" I asked.

"I'm tired of macaroni," he said with a sigh.

"I understand that, believe me, but you've just started learning to cook. I think we should stick with what you know."

"Please, Skye," he begged.

I was tired of macaroni too, so I gave in and walked him through a casserole. He did a pretty good job with it. He was beaming when he told Mom that he had cooked it.

Being grounded wasn't that big of a deal to me. I couldn't drive anyway, and I was still allowed to make phone calls. Steve and I talked a few times, and although I couldn't bring myself to tell him everything, he did seem to understand when I said I had had a bad experience and wanted to take things slow. He said he would still like to take me to a movie when I was allowed to go out again.

Sunny had been doing well in all of his classes but one. Western Civ kept giving him all sorts of problems. I had a hard time just getting him to study with me.

I took Sunny to his swimming lessons, but it depressed me to be around the pool. I had worked so hard and now I couldn't even get in the water. All my teammates, classmates, and even people I didn't really know kept telling me how lucky I was to be a junior, because I could still go to state next year. But I didn't feel lucky. I wanted to go *this* year. As stupid as it was, I felt jealous of Sunny for the first time in my life.

I hung around the lobby while Sunny was swimming, except for when Gail was there. I still felt uncomfortable around her, so I walked over to the park if she was working.

I spent a lot of time just thinking those first few days. Even though the whole business with Mike was supposedly settled, my mind just wouldn't let it go. I kept thinking of what I could've done differently. I could have told him from the beginning I wasn't planning to have sex until I got married. I could have been more open with Jenny or talked to my mom about how nervous he made me. I could have stood my ground the first time we broke up. I could have been less forgiving. Later, I could have told my mom, or Jenny's mom, or even my coach about what Mike had done, instead of ignoring it. If I had done any of those things, my hand might not be in a cast right now. I might still be training for state.

One day Gail caught me by surprise. I had been talking to one of my teammates in the lobby, and she came up and asked if we could talk. I followed her back to the guard room.

"Gail," I blurted out as soon as we walked through the door, "I'm so sorry about everything." She opened her mouth to say something, but it was like the floodgates in my mind had opened. Before I knew it, the whole story poured out.

I told her everything—from my frustration with Sunny to my infatuation with Mike, from the horrifying moments in his room to the humiliating episode at the dance.

"So that's what happened to your hand."

"Yeah."

"Will you be done with the cast and physical therapy by January? That's when we'll be offering lifeguard training."

"You still want me in the class?" I asked in disbelief.

"You said you'll never lie to me again," she said, "and I'll take you at your word."

"Thanks, Gail! Thanks so much!" Impulsively, I hugged her.

She laughed. "You know, you shouldn't be so hard on yourself. Or on Sunny, for that matter." She nodded toward the open door. Across the pool deck we could see Sunny waiting for his lesson to start. "He works hard, and he's a good kid."

"Yeah," I said absently. I walked out on the deck and sat down to watch Sunny's lesson. My mind wandered as I watched him. I wondered if I would still be able to get a college scholarship. I tried to imagine what my life would be like without having Sunny around me every day. I wondered what it would be like for him when I was gone.

Sunny was laughing and happy with the kids in his group. He was really good at helping them, I realized with a shock. A strange thought flashed across my mind: *Does Sunny ever wish for a life of his own? What would that life be like?*

About a week before the Special Olympics, Sunny and I got into a huge fight. Midterm reports were sent home, and he was getting a D in Western Civ.

"What is this?" I demanded, holding the report in his face.

His lower lip started to quiver. "Nothing."

"Nothing? You better believe it's nothing, because a D is what you get when you *do* nothing!"

"It doesn't matter," he muttered.

"It most certainly does," I said. It mattered to me because Mom would think I hadn't been working hard enough with him. And after the swimming lesson fiasco, I was afraid she wouldn't believe me no matter what I said. "What haven't you been showing me?" I asked him.

Sunny got the stubborn look on his face that I knew too well.

"Go get your Western Civ folder."

"No."

"Sunny," I warned, "either go get your folder or tell me what's been going on in class."

He stared at the floor.

"I know it's not your tests and quizzes," I said, "because you've gotten all B's and C's on them."

He still didn't say anything.

I got up and went to his room. He followed me, and started yelling. "You can't go in there without my permithon!"

"Yes, I can. I'm supposed to be helping you with your class work."

I spotted his Western Civ folder, and he tried to beat me to it. I yanked it out of his hands and opened it up. I began to flip through it, but Sunny kept trying to rip it out of my hands. Finally, though, I found what I was looking for.

I pulled out a piece of paper that had Sunny's name on the top. It had about four sentences written in his painstaking handwriting. Beneath that was a two paragraph note written in red from his teacher, asking why he had turned in less than a half page for his four-page report.

"You had a four-page report due?" I asked him. "When was it due?"

"Two weekth ago."

I groaned. Two weeks ago. There was no way I could talk his teacher into taking it this late.

"I can't believe you did this!"

"Tho what?" he snapped at me. "I don't care."

"You will when Mom grounds you."

"Mom won't ground me," he retorted.

"She may not let you swim," I said.

His face fell. "I hate you!" he yelled. "And you don't care about me any-way! You're mad that I get to thwim and you can't!" He shoved me out of his room. I was so shocked I didn't even fight him. He slammed the door in my face, and I could hear him crying on the other side.

Let him cry, I thought. *I'm through trying to help, through being the one who has to do everything for him. Let him learn how hard life really is.*

I waited up for Mom and ambushed her as she came in. I told her my whole story up front, praying she'd believe that I'd been working with him every night, not sure what I'd do if she didn't. Where do you go from the truth?

Fortunately, she believed me. She went in to talk to Sunny, and she did ground him, but not from swimming. He just couldn't watch TV for two weeks.

∾

Mom managed to find a reason to be happy that I broke my hand. Now she didn't have to decide which swim meet to go to. She decided we were all going to the Special Olympics. I found her cheery tone irritating.

"Mom, I still have to go state," I said.

She looked at me. "Why?"

"To support my teammates."

"I think it's more important that you support your brother."

"Mom, I'm tired of always being around him. Besides, it's team policy that we go to the meets as a team."

She sighed. "As I recall, you didn't go to state last year," she said.

"I only went for the finals," I admitted. "But this year I need to be there. I'm still part of the team, even though I can't swim."

"I'm sure your coach will understand."

"Mom, I've worked hard all season. There's a good chance I'll be a co-captain next year. I'm part of the team and I want to go to the meet."

"This is Sunny's first meet."

"He'll be in others."

"Skye! I can't believe how selfish you're being!"

"Well, why not?" I demanded. "I've been swimming for the last three years and you've made it to…what? Two of my meets the whole time? But you get to see Sunny in his first meet. You go watch him, and I'll go to state."

She just sat there for a few moments. I could tell she was really angry. But when she got up to leave the room, she had a disappointed look on her face. I felt kind of rotten, but I told myself I didn't care.

Instead, I got up and called Hannah to see if I could ride with her to state.

"Sure," she said instantly. "But I'm only going for the preliminary heats. I've got to work in the afternoon."

"Okay," I said. "I'm sure I can find another way home."

Each day, as we got closer to the meet, I got more and more upset having to take Sunny to the pool. I was glad I didn't have to go early, in time to see all the fun my teammates were having during the easy week of practice. But I was still angry.

Sunny wasn't quite as happy as I had thought he'd be. He still wasn't talking to me because of the fight about his report, but he also seemed unhappy in general. In fact, he was downright grumpy to everyone a few days before his meet.

When I mentioned that to Mom, she started laughing.

"What? What's so funny about Sunny moping around the house like this?"

Mom caught her breath. "Oh, Skye, he's just copying you."

"What?"

"Whenever you have a big meet coming up, you get all withdrawn."

"I do not!"

She nodded. "Oh, yes, you do. I'm just glad you're not a freshman anymore."

"Why?"

"Because back then, you got withdrawn before *every* meet, so you were pretty much a drag for two solid months of your freshman year." She was still trying to choke back her laughter. "Now I don't need the calendar of meets that you give me. I know when the big ones are coming up, just from your behavior."

"Really?"

Still chuckling, she nodded.

I made a face at her. "Well, if I were you, I wouldn't put up with it."

That made her laugh again. She kissed me on the forehead. "I can't wait till you have kids," she said, walking away.

She always said that when I had done something really good or really stupid. I couldn't tell which one it was this time.

Nov_N_ovember sixth was a typical gray autumn day.

Hannah came to pick me up at almost the same time Sunny and Mom were leaving. I could tell from Mom's face that she really wanted to yell at me, but thankfully she didn't say anything.

"Hey, Sunny, good luck today!" I said as Hannah pulled into the driveway. "I want to hear all the details tonight when I get home."

"Yeah," he said listlessly. "Have fun."

"You too. I know you'll do real well." Before he could answer, I ran out to Hannah's car.

"Good morning," I said, opening the car door.

"What's so good about it?" she asked. "I'm out of bed on a Saturday morning before the sun's up. I'm going to a meet I'm not even swimming in. There's nothing good about it."

I laughed. Hannah never was a morning person.

We drove to school and waited for the bus with the girls who would be swimming. Coach Sullivan said he was glad Hannah and I were there. Finally the bus came and Coach herded the swimmers onto the bus. At the last minute a couple of sophomores showed up, looking for a ride. They got into the backseat of Hannah's car and we followed the bus out to the meet.

When we got there, Hannah and I staked out some good seats in the bleachers above the pool. Not many people were there that early, but I knew that later in the afternoon, the place would be packed.

Christie and Rosa showed up after we had been there for about an hour.

"Wow, Skye. Didn't think we'd see you here today," Christie said.

"Why not?" I demanded. "Aren't I part of the team?"

"Well...well, yeah, of course you are," Christie stammered. "I just don't know if I'd want to be here if I wasn't able to swim. Not after working so hard."

I shrugged. "There's always next year," I said, echoing what everyone else kept saying.

Christie nodded, but she didn't say anything.

"Hey," Rosa said. "I'm going to go get a soda. Anyone else want anything?"

"I'll come with you," I said quickly. I stood up and stretched. "We'll be sitting long enough as it is." I turned to Hannah. "Want to come?"

She shook her head.

"Want anything?"

She shook her head again. "I'm fine."

Rosa and I wandered down to the concession stand, stopping along the way to talk to anybody we knew from other teams. I've always liked swim meets because you actually get the chance to talk to people you compete against. And since most of us had swum on more than one team, we knew a lot of people.

By the time Rosa and I got back to the bleachers, the medley relays were almost over. I wished we had taken a little more time. Now I would have to watch all of the 200-free heats, including the one I was supposed to be in.

Thankfully, Hannah knew me well. She started a random conversation with me and kept me completely entertained. The next time I really looked at the pool, the first three heats of the 200 were over. The slowest time in the last three heats was faster than my best time.

The meet moved very quickly. There was a fifteen-minute intermission instead of diving, because the diving preliminaries had been held the night before. During the intermission, Hannah and I snuck down to the deck. Only coaches and competitors were allowed on the deck, but Hannah and I had figured out how to get down there to see our friends and teammates.

As we walked onto the deck, Hannah turned to me. "I'm going to go say hi to a couple of East swimmers I know."

"Okay," I said, continuing on to our team area.

"Skye!" Deb came up and gave me a big hug. "I didn't know you were coming."

"Wouldn't miss it," I said with a grin. "You looked good today."

Deb grinned back. "Thanks. I dropped almost two full seconds off my best time."

"Cool!"

"I guess Coach does know what he's doing."

"Well, don't tell him that," I said. "We don't need him to start pulling even more attitude with us."

We laughed. Hannah came over, frowning.

"Look out, Skye. I just overheard Coach talking to another coach about kicking nonswimmers off the deck."

"He wouldn't do that to us!"

"Actually," Deb said, "he probably would. They're making a big deal about it this year 'cause it's so crowded."

"We'll just have to stay hidden then," I said with a shrug and a smile.

So we made a game of trying to stay out of Coach's sight while we went around and talked to everyone. It worked for about fifteen minutes. Then, when I went back to talk to Deb again, we got busted.

"Skye?" a deep voice said.

I winced, but put a big grin on my face before I turned around. "Hey, Coach! Hannah and I are here to support our team."

He nodded. "That's great. And we really appreciate you being here. But we need to appreciate you being here in the stands, with the other spectators."

"Coach," Hannah began.

"Don't start," Coach said, shaking his head. "All the coaches agreed, so I have to make sure my team follows the guidelines."

"Okay, we'll go," Hannah said, turning around.

"I'll walk you out," he said.

"That won't be necessary," I said quickly.

"Oh, I think it will be," he said easily. He looked around. "Where's Sunny?" he asked.

I shrugged. "He's…with Mom."

He sighed. "It's amazing, Skye. I was just thinking that this doesn't seem like a real meet, because I can't hear Sunny hollering in the stands. He's been at every meet for the last three years."

"Oh, yeah. But that's because he has to be there."

"He may have to be there, but he cheers as much as he does because he's so proud of you."

I started to feel a little uncomfortable.

Coach shooed us out. "I've got to get back. Second half is about to start. I'll see you at the banquet."

I turned and walked out the pool doors up to the stands above. I tried to get into my friends' conversations, but I really couldn't. I tried to focus on the races, but all I could hear inside my head was "He cheers as much as he does because he's so proud of you."

Hannah turned to me. "Hey, you've got a ride home, right?"

I looked at her. "Are you leaving now?"

"No," she said, shaking her head. "I don't need to leave for another half hour or so. I just wanted to remind you that you need to find a ride home."

"Actually, Hannah, would you mind taking me someplace else? And can we leave right now?"

~

As I opened the outer doors to the city pool, I could hear shouting and whistles from inside the pool area. I walked in quickly. Finding Mom and Sunny would be difficult because there weren't any team or group areas. Everyone was an individual entry here. I checked the pool deck first.

Sandra was there because Sunny had to have a coach to be able to participate. She was standing off to one side, chatting with some other coaches. I worked my way over to her quickly.

She told me that Sunny had already swum two of his three events.

"How did he do?" I asked, hoping my disappointment didn't show.

"He did fine for his first meet," she said, shaking her head, "but he's not happy. He finished last in his heat in the 50 back, and in the 50 free he took second in his heat but didn't place overall."

"How did he look swimming?"

She shrugged. "He's nervous. His stroke reflected that. But he finished both races, which is more than some of the swimmers have done. He should be proud of himself."

"What's his next event?"

"The 100 free. It'll probably be another forty-five minutes before we get to his heat."

"I'm glad I made it in time for that one, at least," I said. "Do you know where my mother is?"

Sandra pointed out where Mom was sitting. I went over quickly and climbed up the bleacher steps. At first Mom didn't see me, but when she did, her eyes opened wide in surprise. Then she glared at me.

"Hi," I said awkwardly, sitting down next to her.

"Hi," she said, turning her eyes back to the pool.

"I hear he did pretty well in the 50 free," I said after a minute.

"Yep."

I sighed. "Mom, I'm sorry. But I'm here now, okay?"

She looked at me out of the corner of her eye. "I guess that's something," she said. She hesitated, then asked, "Skye, you do know that I work two jobs to support you guys, right?"

"Well, yeah," I said, startled.

"You know I don't miss your meets because I'm just out having fun?"

"I know, Mom," I said. "I know you've tried to get to my meets."

"Sometimes you don't act like you know. Or maybe you know, but you don't understand."

"I understand. It just hurts sometimes."

"Sorry, kiddo," she said, putting an arm around my shoulders and leaning her head against mine.

"I'm sorry too," I said, leaning back against her.

"Mr. Bond called. He gave me the number of a therapist."

I sat up in surprise. "What?"

"There's no pressure, Skye. But when you're ready to talk to someone, I want to have help ready."

"Thanks, Mom."

We sat quietly, watching all the commotion around us.

"What did you think of Sunny's events?" I asked.

"I thought he did really well, but I'm thinking that I raised a very poor sport," she said.

"Why?"

"They give ribbons to everyone at the end of each heat," Mom said, "and then they award medals to the top six at the end of the event."

I was nodding. That was standard procedure.

"Well, Sunny finished his race, and the woman who was giving out the ribbons went to give him one. He just pushed past her, completely ignoring the ribbon! I've never seen him do something that rude. I thought he knew better than that."

"Mom, he was just upset. He didn't mean to be rude; he just doesn't want a stupid ribbon when he knows he lost."

She looked at me and arched an eyebrow. "Oh, really? What makes you so sure?"

"Because that's just how I feel when I lose a race," I said.

"But he did really well," she said.

"I'm sure he did," I said. "But he wants to win. There's a difference between doing well and winning."

"Winning isn't everything," Mom began.

"It sure feels like it when you're losing. Especially if you've never really won."

She looked at me for a moment.

I stood up. "Excuse me," I said to the guy sitting next to me, as I started to move past him.

"Where are you going?" Mom asked.

"I'm going to see if I can cheer Sunny up a little bit. I'll be right back."

I wandered down onto the deck. I spotted Sunny, but just as I started toward him, he turned and went the opposite direction. I doubled back, trying to cut him off. This time our eyes met before he turned around and went the other direction. He was intentionally avoiding me.

"Fine," I muttered to myself. "If he doesn't want my help, then I don't want to help him."

I turned around and went back to Mom.

Mom was watching me with a worried look. "What happened?"

"He's sulking."

"You didn't even talk to him. How can you tell?"

"I just can, Mom. He doesn't want to talk to anyone."

She looked at me out of the corner of her eyes. "And how do you know this?"

"Because, when I don't feel I've done my best, I don't want to talk to anyone either."

She shook her head. "Wonderful. Both my children are poor sports."

"We are not. It's just that swimming is a very self-competitive sport. You set a goal for yourself and you get upset if you don't reach it."

We sat through another thirty minutes of races, cheering for everyone. Mom tried several times to get Sunny's attention before she finally gave up and admitted that he was ignoring her too.

"So," she said casually. "Why are you here?"

"I'm here to watch my brother swim."

She smiled and then hugged me. "I'm glad you came. So is Sunny."

I looked at her. "No, he's not."

"Well, he will be."

It was almost time for Sunny's final event. I got up to go to the bathroom. When I came out, I saw Sunny standing just a few feet away with his back to me.

I went up to Sunny and tapped him on the shoulder. He was grinning when he turned around, but when he saw me, his smile faded. His lower lip came out and he stared at the floor.

What I had been about to say evaporated. I had planned on chewing him out for avoiding me and then telling him how he could fix his race. I knew now, though, that that wouldn't work. I took him by the arm and led him into a corner.

I gave him a hug. "You did really well, Sunny," I said warmly.

"You didn't even see me."

"No," I admitted. "But Mom and Sandra said you did great. So I'm looking forward to seeing an awesome race."

"I lost," he said dully.

"That's not what Mom and Sandra said. They said you took second in your heat, and there were people who couldn't even finish."

"It doesn't mean anything."

"Yes, it does, Sunny."

He looked at me doubtfully.

"Besides," I said, "what matters is that you're here and having fun, right? I mean, you weren't even sure you'd get here."

"Yeah," he mumbled. "I guess so."

"And Mom's real proud of you."

"Yeah?"

"Yeah. And so am I."

He looked up. "Really, Skye? You think I did good?"

"I think you did real good," I said, and I hugged him again. "What's more," I said, stepping back, "I think you're going to do even better next time."

"I don't know," he muttered.

"Want some advice?" I asked carefully.

"Sure," he said.

"Don't think of it as a race. Just swim like you're practicing. I bet you'll go faster."

He still looked doubtful. "Why?"

"'Cause sometimes if you try to move your arms and legs too fast in the water, all you do is fight against yourself. Slow, strong strokes will get you farther, especially in a long race. You've got a distance-swimmer stroke, just like me. Keep it smooth, like you do when you practice."

"I look smooth when I'm practicing?"

"Yeah, you sure do."

He smiled, a shy little-boy grin that lit up his whole face. "Okay," he said. "I'll try."

"Good luck," I said, turning to go back to the bleachers.

"Thanks, Skye," he called after me.

I waved and returned to my seat, then gave Mom a play-by-play of the whole conversation.

Mom shook her head. "I knew it," she said.

"Now what?" I asked, irritated. I thought I had done a good thing.

"I knew you had a coaching instinct in you. That's why I asked you to teach him in the first place."

"Thanks, Mom. Next time you're going to send me on a guilt trip, give me a little warning so I can pack a lunch."

She nodded. She was watching Sunny begin pacing behind his lane again. After a few moments she shook her head. "While you were talking to him, why didn't you tell him to stop doing that? Just watching him is making me nervous."

I laughed self-consciously. I almost told her that it was my way of getting ready for a race that he was imitating, but she might have thought I was upset that she didn't already know that.

Mom nudged me. "How do you think he'll do this time?"

I shook my head. "This race is twice as long as the last two."

Mom made a face. "Oh, no."

"Yeah. You could say that."

The swimmers from the previous heat climbed out, and the starter called Sunny's heat to the blocks. Sunny stepped up, shaking out his arms in an eerie likeness of me. I never thought we'd ever have anything in common

The swimmers took their marks, and then they were off. Sunny's start was the fastest, but he did a belly flop.

When he came up, he was clearly in the lead. His first few strokes were awkward. They were short and choppy, almost panicky. But then he started to stretch out, started to get smooth.

He held the lead for the whole first length. He reached out, grabbed the wall, and pushed off as quickly as he could. His lead only increased during the second length.

"Come on, Sunny!" Mom hollered next to me. "Yeah, Sunny!"

I stayed quiet, watching him swim. His strokes were long and powerful. He had a good rhythm, and he was kicking consistently. Each pull increased his lead. He was slicing easily through the water; he was flying.

He started the third length and I couldn't see any signs of fatigue; the strokes looked the same. He was breathing every other stroke, using a tight turn of his head instead of rolling over on his back like his competitors. But coming off his last turn, he started to fall apart. I could see the strokes getting sloppier.

"Come on, Sunny," I murmured. "Hang in there, Sunny, you've got it, just finish tough."

He did. His strokes kept getting worse and I could almost feel his fatigue. But he finished tough. He completed the race, which was more than the swimmers in two of the lanes could say. And he finished almost a length in front of everyone else.

Mom and I screamed and yelled. He stood up and looked behind him, and the smile that spread across his face could have lit up the whole pool area if the electricity had gone out.

He climbed out of the pool, and we waited for him to look our way or come see us.

Mom started laughing. "I wish I could have videotaped you. I would love for you to see yourself."

I looked at her. "See what? I saw you screaming your head off; at least I wasn't doing that."

"No," Mom agreed. "You weren't screaming. You were just trying to push him to the finish from here."

"What? What are you talking about?"

"I'm talking about this," Mom said, and she began to rock back and forth on the bench, mumbling, "Come on, Sunny, come on."

"I did not—" I began to protest, even as I realized that I had.

Mom was laughing at me.

"I think you were probably more into his race than he was, Skye," Mom said.

"Where is he?" I asked, looking across the pool for him.

I finally located him. I watched him for a minute before he glanced in our direction. I waved. He shook his head.

I groaned.

"What?" Mom asked.

"Sunny's over there and he still won't come here."

"What's wrong this time?"

"I have no idea," I said. But I thought I did. Sunny was watching the other races intently, checking the clock every time a heat finished. Sandra was with him, and he kept nodding at what she said.

"He won the race," Mom said, after we had been watching him for a minute. "What more does he want?"

"He didn't win the race, he won his heat. He wants to win the race."

"What was his time?" Mom asked me, watching the scoreboard as it flashed competitors' times.

"I didn't even look," I admitted.

When the last heat of the 100 finished, Sandra started jumping up and down. Sunny was shaking his head. Even from across the pool I could read that body language. Sandra was pleased with the place he had taken; Sunny wasn't.

I knew I had to go talk to him. I knew he was hurting and I knew exactly how he felt. Quickly I got up and worked my way down through the bleachers to the pool deck. I was so intent on getting to the other side of the pool that I really wasn't watching where I was going. He was almost completely past me before I realized he was walking toward our seats in the bleachers.

"Sunny!"

He turned. I could tell from his red-rimmed eyes that he had been crying again.

"Where are you going?"

He leaned his head toward the officials' table. "They're doing the awards ceremony."

I listened. I could barely hear the announcer over the rumbling of the crowd. He was calling off the final standings for the 100 free. I nodded, and turned to follow Sunny through the crowd. We stopped a few feet away from the awards table.

I kept listening, ready to burst into applause and show Sunny how proud I was of him, no matter what place he took. I kept waiting. Tenth place, seventh place, fifth, fourth. I turned to look at Sunny, who was calmly watching the announcer. He had taken third? No.

"And in second place, Abraham Johnson."

It took Sunny stepping forward for me to realize that he had registered with his real name instead of his nickname, and that he had taken second. I began clapping and shouting as loud as I could, and I threw in some really obnoxious whistles too.

He collected his medal and turned back to me. He was crying again.

"Sunny," I called over all the applause. "Why are you crying? You did so well! Look at you, you took second place!"

He lifted the ribbon and settled the medal over my head.

"What are you doing?" I asked in confusion.

He was still crying. "I know you would have done better than second at state," he said. "But you can have my medal anyway."

I was floored. I began shaking my head. The fact that I wouldn't have even placed at state ran briefly through my mind, but I knew this was not the time to say that. He wouldn't believe me anyway. For some reason, he thought I was great.

"Oh, no, Sunny, I can't take this. I didn't do anything to deserve this. I did everything not to deserve this!" Tears were rolling down my face too.

I hugged him and he hugged back hard.

I had never felt closer to him, had never felt more like a sister to him, than I did then, and it was at the time that I least deserved it. It dawned on me that in spite of everything, he would forgive me because he loved me.

I loved him too.